The
COLOR
of Your Tears

BARBARA COMBS WILLIAMS

The Color of Your Tears

Copyright © 2018 by Barbara Combs Williams

A Remember Too Design

ISBN 978-1-7336352-0-2

Thank You!

I want to thank so many people for helping me make *The Color of Your Tears* possible. There is of course my wonderful husband Heyward, who without his influence I never would have even started writing.

Thanks to our daughter Nicole who gave me so much help with understanding millennials and what makes them tick.

Then there are my beta readers who without their help this book would be so much nonsense. If I start naming them I would surely miss a name and whew, trouble would ensue. So you know who you are, sisters of my blood and sister friends.

And of course my editor Candice, who gave me so much sound advice and helped me through this entire process.

And be on the lookout for my next book, *Crystal Clear - Chrystal's Story.*

Thank you all from the bottom of my heart!
Barbara @ www.BarbaraCombsWilliams.com

1

What's the color of your tears?
Pooling in the depths of your eyes
Dismal grays mocking silent fears
Clogged throats and desperate cries

Wednesday night – three days before wedding

Jackie Mattock locked herself inside the tiled bathroom adjoining her master bedroom and sat down on the floor. Lavender tears streamed down her puffy cheeks and pooled into the soft folds around what used to be her sleek collarbones. A strange gurgling sound drummed loudly in her ears. To her further distress and humiliation, she realized the sounds were coming from her. Everything was in such a total mess that she didn't know what to do now. She had tried everything to get her oldest child, Chrystal, to see reason, but as Jackie knew, neither reason nor sanity was Chrystal's middle name.

This should have been one of the happiest times in a mother's life. Jackie's son was getting married to a great girl who was his whole world. The wedding would take place on Saturday, just three days away. Summer was shining bright with the promise of a beautiful day for the wedding. But here it was Wednesday night and Chrystal threatened to destroy the whole thing just because it wasn't about her. Jackie couldn't believe Chrystal had come all this way to Decatur, and at this time of night, to continue to make Jackie's life a misery.

"Oh Lord," she prayed, "I know I have failed at so many things in my life." She thought of her disastrous marriage to Jimmy, who after fifteen years and two children decided he didn't really want a wife or children. Then there was Chrystal who always found a way to work on her last nerves. "If you will just grant me this one blessing, I will do whatever is in my power to be the person you have destined me to be. Grant me the strength and the determination to survive this fight that I know is ever growing around me. Lighten my burden and give me the sense to know what to do when the time comes. Let my children's hearts be full of gentleness and kindness. Lead them in the right path and give them the knowledge to know when you are leading them and the sense to follow you. I know all things are done in your time, but please, I need this now, as quickly as possible, before I have to kill my oldest child. I ask for this in Jesus's name. Amen."

Jackie didn't know if God heard her prayer or not, but she did feel a little better and got up from where she lay huddled up against the bathtub. She wasn't an overly religious woman, and at forty-nine and divorced, she didn't really expect any miracle to suddenly manifest itself for her. But why not? Nothing else was working, so what was there to lose in appealing to the Lord?

She got up stiffly from the floor. Her faded housedress bunched around her thighs, the fabric straining against her hips. She needed to get rid of the old thing, too tight these days, but like most things in her life, she held on to it for the wrong reasons. Her knees ached from where she had bent down to lie on the cool tile, and her hip would probably have a bruise from where she flung herself against the bathroom door in anger to close it before Chrystal could follow her into the room.

Okay, let me get myself together before those babies start pounding on the door, looking for Grandma Jack, she thought. *I'll just cool my burning* cheeks with a little water and—Oh Lord! Look at my eyes. Can't hide that red. Where's the eye drops that's supposed to get the red out? And my hair, flat on one side and drooping on the other. Good thing my natural style can take a lot of laying around on the floor. I'll just pull a little here and tug some there, and I think I can pass for a respectable, intelligent, middle-aged grandmother now.

I don't know why I let her get to me every time, but that girl just makes me so mad. Why does she always have to be so much trouble? She has the nerve to come here with all those babies and demand that I do something about them. I didn't tell her to lie down with God only knows who and have all those babies one after the other. Here she comes with four–and-half-year-old Jewel, three-year-old Oro and bringing up the rear, Jade at eighteen months. And why did she give those babies such stupid names anyway. Where in the world did she get that stuff from? Lord oh Lord, where did I go wrong with her?

Each child had the look of Chrystal, and to an extent of Jackie herself, about them. But in each child, it was plain to see there loomed a different daddy. Jackie had her suspicions about the fathers. Chrystal never confirmed to her any of the boys or men she had been involved with. She was stubborn personified.

Jewel almost had an Asian look about her. Her little eyes were slanted and her curly-topped head of hair was much finer than Chrystal's and reddish in color. Jackie thought maybe Jewel's father was a boy whose mother was Korean and daddy was black. He had lived one street over, and Chrystal was sweet on him once. What was his name? Jeremy, or Jason, or something like that.

Oro, on the other hand, looked just the opposite. He was a milk chocolate color, but his hair was jet black, long, and wavy. Maybe his daddy was the son of the East Indian guy who owned the convenience store down the street. Chrystal used to hang around that convenience store all the time, getting free drinks and stuff. She was always talking about Omar, how cute he was and so nice to her and Jewel when they went into the store.

Now Jade, Jackie didn't have any idea who that baby's daddy was. Jade, bless her heart, looked like somebody had given Chrystal the wrong baby at the hospital. Jade could have been a white woman's child, what with her gray eyes and light brown wavy hair. But Jackie loved them all the same, no matter their parentage. Those babies had no pick in the matter. She just wished they weren't such a stereotype of the perfectly dysfunctional family.

But who was to blame for Chrystal's behavior anyway? Jackie didn't notice Chrystal was pregnant with Jewel until Chrystal was seven months along. Even after Jewel was born, no daddy showed up to claim her. Jackie pressured Chrystal before and after the birth as to the father of Jewel, but stubborn Chrystal wouldn't budge and gave up no information. So on Jewel's birth certificate, there was no father acknowledged.

Still, Jackie thought she did everything in her power to help. She babysat when she could so Chrystal could get her GED. Jackie didn't want her daughter to miss out on opportunities for good jobs because of not finishing high school. Chrystal had never been very studious and her attitude seriously needed adjusting, but Jackie constantly pushed her to get it done. Jackie had also made their home as cozy as possible with a newborn to care for. Never in her wildest dreams would she have thought she would be a grandmother to three little ones. Chrystal's behavior was probably the second biggest disappointment of Jackie's life.

She often wondered what Royce thought about it all. His older sister, who he should be looking up to, had a baby out of wedlock, and no one came to claim the baby. But Royce never said a word to her about it. He would help out whenever he could, but he never spoke on it. He would just hold the baby, gently stroking her fuzzy head of hair. He would feed her and sing to her in his rapidly changing voice, but diapering was left up to Jackie or Chrystal. It almost seemed as if he took on the role of the missing daddy, and he was only a child himself.

At the best of times Chrystal was hard to get along with, but now she was even more difficult and withdrawn from both her and Royce. Of course, that made Jackie feel even guiltier, and she wondered at her own lack of maternal feelings toward Chrystal.

Just before Oro was born Chrystal had decided she needed to be out on her own. Jackie half-heartily tried to talk her out of it, but Chrystal was adamant that she needed her own space. Deep down, Jackie wanted her to move out, but she tried not to show it. A sullen Chrystal and a crying baby were not in the picture she had painted for herself. Her little piece of sanity and the tenuous peace in her heart were the most important things in her life now. Chrystal threatened that with all her theatrics. What Jackie wanted most in life she could never have, and Chrystal's very presence brought back too many painful memories. She often felt Chrystal saw through her act.

Jackie was so happy when Chrystal and her childhood girlfriend Chantrelle moved into subsidized housing together. Chantrelle had a one-year-old son named Christian, but unlike Chrystal, she actually seemed to be getting her act together. The two families shared a rental over in Grant Park, and remarkably, they got along well together. Jackie never wanted to go over there though because Chrystal's part of the house looked like a war zone. Dirty clothes and toys covered every surface. Jackie never understood how Chrystal could actually lay her head down in that filth. Even though they were a handful, she much preferred to babysit the kids in her own house, in Decatur, when she couldn't get out of it.

Although they were about as opposite as opposites could get, Chrystal and Chantrelle still shared the rental. Whereas Chrystal went on to three kids in all, Chantrelle stopped with Christian. Chantrelle even had a car so they could get around, and unlike Chrystal, she knew who her baby-daddy was and how to get him to pay up child support.

Chantrelle and Chrystal both worked at the same nursing home, but on different shifts. Both Jackie and Chantrelle's mother, Clara, bent over backwards to help their daughters and grandchildren. But best of all, the grandmothers had each other's backs and really were good support for each other's children.

～

Jackie's mind was so muddled now that she couldn't focus on any one thought, much less what was going on in her house. The babies were family, and she loved them with all her heart, but their mother—where had Jackie gone wrong? She thought back to what seemed like hours ago, but was in reality just ten minutes.

Chrystal came busting through the door hollering, "Mom, I need you to keep the kids, 'cause I'm hooking up with this guy I met at the club who's gonna get me in on a video. I know you don't think I have talent, but Smoke knows I got it going on and my time is now, and he's blowing up too as a producer and—whatever, just keep these loud grandchildren of yours cause I got to dip." Chrystal raced through her monologue as if she was afraid Jackie would disappear before she could finish. She ushered all the kids in and directed them to the sofa, holding on to the youngest as she paced back and forth with their tote bag. Suddenly she placed the baby on the sofa while dumping the kids' little belongings beside her.

Chrystal turned from Jackie to race out the door, but Jackie grabbed at her arm and stopped her. She didn't have much to grab on to. Chrystal always wore the skimpiest things she could find. Tonight she had on low-riding jeans, a neon-green tube top, and chunky stacked heels. Jackie thought those things were out of style, but again, what did she know about today's styles? She had to give it to Chrystal though; after three kids in a row, the girl still had a perfect body, and she could get away with wearing much of nothing, although Jackie would never tell her that.

Chrystal had a beautiful face with pecan brown skin and light brown eyes. Jackie always thought Chrystal looked just like her daddy. Beautiful smiling eyes, gorgeous body, if only she had the attitude to go along with it. Chrystal drew men to her like the proverbial bees to honey. But following the typical stereotype, they were all thugs, hoods, and no-accounts. Nothing Jackie did deterred Chrystal from her path. She was determined to choose the rockiest, dirtiest unpaved road to travel with what Jackie considered to be the lowest bridge trolls as companions.

"Where the hell do you think you're going? These are your children and not my responsibility. I am the grandmother. You are their mama. They need you. You can't just run away with some guy you just met. Girl, are you crazy? I thought I raised you better than that. You need to—"

"See. That's the way it's always been. You never had time for me and what I was going through. You never loved me, and you don't care about what happens to your own damn grandchildren."

"Chrystal, you must have lost what little mind you have. You know better than to talk to me like that. I know you think you grown, and at twenty-three with three kids, you should be, but Chrystal, you're not thinking of them or what's best for you. What do you know about some guy with a crazy name, and why would he want to put you in a video? You don't dance or sing, so exactly what talent are you talking about?"

"You ain't never tried to help me, and all I ask you to do is one little favor, and you act like I'm not even your child and you can't do it." Chrystal tossed her long hair as she turned as if to go, but she was really looking at her cell phone.

"And what about your job at the center? You can't keep taking time off. You know you need that nursing assistant job. Besides, I got to work tomorrow, and I have no way to take care of three kids, even if they are my grandchildren. You just can't leave them as if they were garbage at the curb."

"What do you care about my job? I got them stupid people at the center eating out of my hand. They not only gave me three days off, but they're gonna change my shift when I get back so I can get paid more money, so don't you worry none about my job. Besides them old people are gonna die whether I'm there or not to change their damn adult diapers."

"Please don't talk about those people like that. I know you have more compassion than that. Besides, you know Royce's wedding is Saturday and there's a lot to do before then. What about Chantrelle or her mom? Can't they keep the kids as usual? Why don't you just—?"

"Chantrelle has the flu, and she's staying over at her mom's place. I don't want my kids around all that stuff. You know how easy it is for Jade to get sick."

Chrystal tried to shake off the baby's hand as Jade clutched at her legs. "You know it's always about Royce with you anyway. I guess I need to get Royce to ask you something, and then you'll do it. I bet if Royce asked you to look after his girlfriend's baby, you would just jump at that and gobble that little heifer's kid up like sugar, and she ain't even related to you."

"I don't even know what you're talking about. Royce's fiancée, Jessica, not *heifer*, doesn't even have a baby, so how could I gobble her up like sugar? You're just talking nonsense."

Jackie was so confused by Chrystal's babble that she didn't know if she was coming or going, and frankly at that point, she just didn't care. She was tired of the whole conversation already. Chrystal always made her blood boil. Why was Chrystal always so demanding and angry at the same time? Had she Jackie, made Chrystal into this terrible selfish person?

The kids were all looking at the crazy scene unfolding before them. The oldest, Jewel, had some understanding of what was going on. She could tell her mama was trying to leave without them and started in on a low, slow, but steady whine. Jackie knew it wouldn't be long before the other two, Oro and Jade, started in also, and her nerves just couldn't take that. She loved her grandkids and knew it wasn't their fault that their mother was acting the fool once again, but she just couldn't keep them. They were usually good babies, but what the oldest did so did the other two, and right now was not the time to have her house torn apart with all their childish ways. Chrystal even had the nerve to have the youngest two dressed in their pajamas, like they were ready to be put down to bed in her house.

Jewel was gearing up for a really good tantrum. Jackie could tell by the way the child started doing that manic little tap dancing on her wood floor with those hard-bottomed Dora the Explorer shoes Jackie had bought her. Why did Chrystal have to come now of all nights and, as usual, be so selfish and act so crazy?

"I just want you to keep them for a couple of days, and you act like I asked you for the freaking moon. I'm just going to Miami for a little while. Like I said, this guy Smoke is really dope right now, and I got to get in on some of this cheese before it's over." Chrystal said all this while reaching into the bag she'd brought over and trying to pull out some pajamas to put on Jewel.

"I don't know about this. It doesn't feel right. I want to help, and you know I've always tried to do whatever I could for you. When your father left us all, and you were just twelve, I did everything I could to be both mother and father to you and your brother."

"See you can stop right there. Daddy left *you*! And there's no way you've ever been mother and father to me. I know for a fact that Daddy loves me and my kids."

"Well, I have tried my best. Who came to your school to support everything you were involved in from band to soccer? It damn sure wasn't your daddy. I'm the one who put up with every teacher who said you were full of anger and in denial. I stood up to every one of them and defended your actions and behavior, even when I knew in my heart that you did most of those things they said you did. Yes, I know I didn't do everything you asked, how would I? Some of those things you wanted to do were just crazy and full of silly, childish anger.

"I have helped with every one of the kids, while trying to respect your privacy. I knew better than to let you have your own way. These children need a daddy, and you just keep on popping them out like a vending machine."

Jackie took a deep breath and continued before Chrystal could dispute her. "And what about your little episode with the police and that mess that went down? Who was right there with you, pleading with that judge, borrowing everything I could to get you out? That wasn't your daddy either. And now you have the nerve to stand there and say I never did anything for you! You ask me to do something for you that you know is unreasonable, and you expect me to just drop everything that's in the works to let you go off on some whim!"

Jackie could feel her blood pressure going higher and higher. If she wasn't careful, she would really blow a fuse this time. The kids looked on with real fright in their eyes. Their mother was acting like a fool, and Grandma wasn't doing too much better, but what was she to do? She couldn't let Chrystal mess everything up once again.

Chrystal was the master at manipulation. She knew exactly how to get to Jackie every time. Because it wasn't about what Jackie wouldn't do for her now. Instead, it was always about how Jackie drove her precious daddy away.

Jackie doubted anything she did for Chrystal would ever be enough. Guilt was riding her. What good mother would have let her daughter get pregnant at seventeen, and keep having baby after baby with anybody who looked at her, and never do anything to stop it?

Jackie felt it was all her fault that Chrystal was the way she was. She never thought she was a good mother, and maybe God was punishing her because of her failure to recognize that her husband Jimmy was in love with someone else and ignored his wife and children. She in turn was so consumed with trying to make it all work that she hadn't given her children the attention they needed, especially Chrystal.

She had never ever told her children the real reason she and their father divorced. Shame and embarrassment over her inability to keep her man were the main reasons and they were way too young to understand anyway. But she didn't want everyone else to look at her with pity in their eyes. To most people the breakup only confirmed that Jackie didn't know what to do with a good man.

Jackie's own mother, Sylvia Stinson (better known to everyone in Boulevard Heights as Ms. Sylvi) had told her that Chrystal wasn't nothing but "the devil tied up in the package of a sweet looking little baby girl." This she knew after keeping the baby for a night once when Chrystal was just three months old.

Twenty-three years ago

Jackie had begged her mom for a night alone to have dinner out and spend some quiet time with Jimmy. To be honest, it seemed everything depended on this one night. Jimmy hadn't touched her since Chrystal was born, and Jackie felt he wasn't about to, but she was determined to get their love life back on track.

Really, Jimmy hadn't touched her much when she was pregnant with Chrystal either. Being naïve, Jackie thought he just didn't want to hurt her, even though she kept telling him she was all right and the doctor said they could have sex as long as she was comfortable. Apparently, she wasn't the one who was uncomfortable.

They were only into the entrée portion of their meal at a prime steakhouse when Jackie felt something strange go all over her. She had broken out in a cold sweat. She stopped eating and made an excuse to go the ladies room. Lucky for her, the phones were right outside, and she was able to call Ms. Sylvi. "Mom, I just got a strange feeling. Is everything all right?" She already knew the answer since she could hear the screaming from Chrystal through the phone, but she asked anyway.

"You and Jimmy need to come and get this demon child," her mother said. Since the minute you all drove off, this baby has been crying herself to death and raising my blood pressure to stroke level. Here, Buddy, hold this baby while I talk to Jackie."

"Mom, what happened? She was asleep when we left and should have stayed that way for hours," said Jackie with big wet tears in her eyes.

"Well, I don't know but one thing. This baby won't take anything from me. She won't eat. I changed her diapers; I sang to her, I rocked her. Nothing I do makes a difference. She is the orneriest little thing I've ever seen. Nothing like you at that age or your sister Nancy neither. She's looking at me now with those sparkling eyes full of tears, like I slapped her or something. I have never seen a look on a baby's face like that before. Here. Wait a minute. Your daddy wants to talk to you."

Jackie knew she needed to get to her mom's house before Ms. Sylvi really did have a stroke. Her mother wasn't that old or infirm, but she liked to pretend she was sometimes just for the drama. Ms. Sylvi worked at Macy's and had for most of her adult life. She was used to irate customers and could handle the stress.

Jackie hated for the one night she had been planning on and needed so badly to end so soon, and she knew she would never get her mom to babysit little Chrystal again. Just then, an older white woman came out of the rest room and looked directly at her. Jackie knew people could probably hear her conversation, but at that point, she just didn't care. She braced herself for some criticism from the woman but was so surprised when the lady said, "Oh, honey, I hope everything's all right. I'm going to pray for you," and patted her on the back. All Jackie could do was lay her head against the wall.

"Hello, Jackie," said her dad, Buddy. "You take your time and don't rush around doing something foolish. Your mom and I will be fine until you get here. And don't let your mom fool you. It ain't that bad." Buddy was also used to his wife's theatrics. He also worked for the Atlanta water department and had heard every excuse there was as to what was wrong with people's water meters. He had learned how to have a lot of patience.

"Okay, Daddy. We'll be right there. Just give us an hour to wrap up this food and get out of Buckhead."

Jackie's mother got back on the phone.

"I'm sorry, Mom. I really am."

"I'm sorry too baby and I tried everything I knew how, but this child wants you and Jimmy, not me and Buddy. She just won't be happy until then." Unfortunately, Jackie felt her mother was all too correct. Well, not about Chrystal wanting her because she definitely seemed to be a daddy's girl.

Jackie cried all the way back to the table. Big white tear streaks were painted on her cheeks. Jimmy looked at her curiously as she sat down. "What's the matter, baby? Why are you crying? Is my company that bad?"

Jackie picked up her napkin and tried to dab at her eyes and cheeks. Her hands shook so much she almost dropped the napkin to the floor. "No, nothing like that, but I just talked to Mom and Chrystal seems to be sick. She wants us to come back and get her. Let's just get this food to go and call it a night."

"Okay baby, let's get going. And Jackie, don't worry about Chrystal. I'm sure she's fine. It's the first time we've been away from her. She probably just woke up and was confused. You know my little princess is probably just missing us."

Sure, Jackie thought to herself. *I'm sure Chrystal is fine, but what about me? I'm missing something too, and having Chrystal crying in the next room is not going to let me get it. I can't take too much more of this pent up frustration. What kind of marriage have I got myself into?*

And then, I hungered for all of you mightily
I imagined all the touches I could give
If only you let you, if only I would, if only we dared
Together we could soar on wings of spun gold

∽

Jackie snapped her mind back to the present and tried to jump two steps ahead of Chrystal and not let her daughter catch her in a vulnerable position. She noticed that Jewel, followed closely by Oro and Jade, came and grabbed her mother's leg. Jackie watched as her grandchildren practically jumped on their mama and began really crying and whining.

"Mama, don't go. Don't leave us with Grandma Jack. Please, mama. I'll be a good girl. Please!" said Jewel as she hugged Chrystal tighter. Jackie just knew Jewel would eventually wet herself with all the excitement going on. All Jackie needed was a little pissy girl to add to the confusion.

Little Oro decided it was time for him to do as his big sister did and latched on to Chrystal's ankle and wouldn't let go. "Ma, ma, mama, I good boy, I good boy," he said. And poor Jade tripped and fell over her brother and sister, sat down heavily on the floor, and cried.

"Y'all kids better sit down and stop acting the fool," yelled Chrystal as she tenderly picked up Jade and placed her on the couch.

"You always pull that old crap out your ass every time I ask you to do me a favor. I'm sick and tired of hearing about what I did or didn't do in school. I know what I know. You're the reason Daddy left me. You and only you sent him away. You're the one who couldn't handle it. If I got over it, then you sure need to. When will that happen? Besides, I ain't even thinking about that mess from back then. All you do is talk about the same old stuff. That's old news. Can't you forget about that and get a life?" Chrystal turned back to her children. "I told you kids to sit down and shut up. I have had just about enough of all of y'all."

Chrystal's words hurt more than Jackie wanted to admit. But she couldn't let Chrystal guilt her into doing something she knew she wasn't prepared for. She knew letting Chrystal leave her with those kids was not the best thing for Chrystal or the kids and certainly not for her, but what was she to do? She tried another tactic and prayed it would work.

"Chrystal, why don't you get your new friend to put off the trip for a few days, until after the wedding, and then I'll keep them for you? I can get your Aunt Nancy to come over and help. Maybe even your Grandma Sylvi could help out too. You know how the kids love their great-granny. Three little ones is a lot to handle for me right now."

Chrystal paced back and forth, burning a track on her floors, but Jackie continued anyway. "You know your aunt just retired from teaching, and she always knows how to handle the kids. She's looking for some excitement for the summer. We'll get their favorite toys to play with, and I don't think you have enough diapers for Oro and Jade for a long stay anyway."

Jackie tried to gauge Chrystal's mood, hoping she would consent. "That way everybody gets what they want. You see the kids are all upset, and if you leave them now, nobody will get any rest. You know my blood pressure is sky high and all that noise they're making isn't helping my headache any." Jackie thought she had covered everything and hoped it would work. She couldn't have been more wrong.

Chrystal exploded as if hit by dynamite. "Grandma Sylvi is ancient and demented! Aunt Nancy is almost senile too. What good is she going to do me? She ain't never had any children and don't know the first thing about babies. She's just a crazy old woman and can't even remember what day of the week it is. She had to retire or the people at that school were gonna drag her old funky butt out by her nappy hair. I wouldn't trust her around my kids, and you know that!"

At that moment, Jackie knew her mother was right when she said Chrystal was a demon child. Not that she had ever had any doubts. "I can't believe you would talk about your grandmother and auntie that way. They have always been there for you, and you just don't understand—"

Chrystal went on as if her mother hadn't even spoken. "You ain't got to go to work tomorrow. Just call that man and tell him the kids are sick or something. You know you could do that if you really wanted to and everything would be fine at your job. Besides, Smoke can't put off the video shoot because everything is all planned and I got to go now."

Chrystal picked up her bag and slung it over her shoulder. "Get off my ankle, Oro, and go over there by your sister and sit down. Jewel, stop all that screaming, wipe your nose, and go and sit down too. Your grandma ain't gonna want to keep you if y'all keep acting up. I said shut up, all of you, and stop acting like y'all ain't got no sense."

To Jackie, Chrystal said, "I can't believe you expect me to give up my chance at some happiness. Put off my trip, you must be damn senile too."

Jackie was so hurt by the angry words Chrystal threw at her. She knew there was no reasoning with her, and mustering up as much dignity as she could, she walked out of her great room, towards her bedroom at the back of the house.

"Mom, where are you going? Are you going to keep your grand-children or not? I said get off me, Oro, and sit down. Mom, wait. I need to know."

Jackie had walked faster to her room. She knew if she didn't get away from Chrystal and all that noise from the children, she would really start to act crazy. She had run into the bathroom with Chrystal on her heels and slammed the door in her face.

Now here she stood with her back literally against the wall. Jackie washed her face again in cold water. Her head was absolutely pounding, and she felt dizzy and lightheaded. She could hear Chrystal and the kids outside the door. Chrystal was trying to get Jewel to ask her "nicely" to come out and play with them. Chrystal would start in with more threats of just leaving the kids if she didn't come out soon.

Jackie had been through this with her daughter before. She remembered the time a few months after little Oro was born. Chrystal had carried a bundle in her arms and dragging a whimpering Jewel, tripping and falling over everything because she was new to walking. She'd dropped them both in the middle of the couch. She needed time to get everything straight with Oro's father and the kids would just get in the way until she did had been her reply to "What in God's name are you doing here in this weather?" Jackie had kept them both for over a week; she had used her vacation time until Chrystal came to her senses and came back and picked them up. Apparently she couldn't get that baby-daddy straight.

Then there was the time right after Jade had just turned six months old. Chrystal, excited about a new man in her life, said she just needed a few weeks to get to know him better and "Mom, please just keep the kids for a little while until me and Quincy get to that place in our relationship. I don't want the kids to scare him off. He's really cool, and he's going to be the next great NBA star. Just wait and see." Well, she had done that, since Chrystal had actually asked before dumping the kids on her. Unfortunately, the NBA contract didn't come through, and as the contract went so went Chrystal's interest in Quincy. Jackie guessed "that place" had disappeared also.

"Grandma Jack, please come out and see what I can do." That was Jewel doing as her mother said.

"Okay, don't break the door down. I'm coming out in just a second. Hold on."

Jackie dried her lavender tears, wiped her face again with the cool washcloth, and said another silent prayer. *Lord, I believe you will put the words in my mouth that I need to tell my daughter. I know you know all, and everything will be fine in its own time. Please give me strength to endure whatever may come.*

Jackie opened the bathroom door and silently walked out into a sight that would normally have made her want to tear her hair out.

There was Chrystal lying across her bed with Jewel jumping up and down on her pillows with those hard, dusty shoes on. She noticed Chrystal had given the kids her last banana, and Oro and Jade were giggling over at the window taking their spitty banana hands from their mouths and wiping them all over the clear window pane. Jewel was just about to lean down and grab a handful of Jackie's multicolored coverlet up to her banana smeared face. How many times had she told Chrystal not to put the kids on her bed with food? And now look at the mess they were making. She just didn't care or think about anyone but herself.

Nevertheless, Jackie plunged on with what she needed to say. "Chrystal, you're right. Go on and get your chance at stardom. I don't want to mess that up for you. I can keep the kids, and we'll just work something out with your aunt Nancy. I'll call her right now. Everything will be fine. But please promise me you'll be careful. I've heard nothing but horror stories about these video shoots." There, she had said it; she couldn't believe the Lord had put those words in her mouth. But hadn't she prayed for the right words?

Without even looking up from playing with her phone, Chrystal said, "Oh, Mom, I just got a text from Smoke and he said the shoot has been postponed until next week. I don't need you to keep the kids after all. I don't know why you were getting so worked up anyway. All that crying and moaning you were doing in the bathroom was getting on my nerves and scaring the kids. Anyway, my new man will take care of me and my kids. You don't have to worry about us. Come on, kids. Let's give Grandma Jackie her space back. She looks like she needs to lie down. Get off that window Oro, and get your sister. Jewel, come on. Smoke is coming to pick us up."

Chrystal tossed her long black weave over her shoulder and walked out of the bedroom without a backwards glance. She looked just like a mother duck with all her little mismatched ducklings following in a row. The thought almost made Jackie smile. She still couldn't understand why her daughter kept putting all that fake hair in her head when she had beautiful shoulder-length hair, but worse than that, she couldn't understand how the girl went from one extreme to the other in the blink of eye. Was she the one who was crazy, or was Chrystal just that smart?

 **2**

What's the color of your tears?
Dingy, tan, cascading swollen falls
Grinding, stripped out rusty gears
Pretending to answer futile calls

Jackie sat down on her bed after Chrystal and the kids left out of the room. She could hear Chrystal talking to them in the hallway about where they were going. She just couldn't understand why Chrystal was the way she was. She knew motherhood had changed her significantly but Chrystal still seemed unfazed. Had she, Jackie been that terrible a mother? After the breakup with Jimmy, she had done everything in her power to do right by Chrystal and Royce. Chrystal had been devastated by the divorce, and Jackie knew Chrystal blamed her for everything.

They had all gone to counseling and talked about their feelings with the therapist her employee assistance program provided. The therapist didn't tell her anything she didn't already know about Chrystal. He did say Chrystal was searching for a father figure unlike the one who had betrayed her trust and love. He also said she would probably act out this scenario of going from boy to boy, man to man, time and again until she replaced him. And that might be never. "Sometimes they have to hit the wall a few times," the therapist said, "before they realize the futility of it." Thankfully she didn't know at the time that Chrystal would hit the wall three times and still wouldn't seem to get the big picture.

In the sessions, Jackie talked very little about her feelings. She was more concerned about her children, especially Royce. She never let on that the hole she had crawled into was deeper and wider than anything she could have ever imagined. She suppressed her feelings and channeled all her emotions into taking care of Chrystal and Royce. Jackie was determined that they would never suffer from the lack of love from their father. She would just have to be both mother and father to her children since their father didn't want to be involved in their lives anymore.

Royce seldom talked about his dad to her. He would go with Jimmy when he came to pick the children up on some infrequent weekend, but he didn't act like he was overjoyed to do it. Whereas Chrystal was usually out the door the minute Jimmy pulled into the driveway, Royce talked even less when he came back from those weekends with his father. He was more withdrawn and clung to Jackie like a shadow. She wondered what actually occurred on those weekends but was too afraid to ask.

Chrystal talked excessively about her father after they returned home. Jackie wanted to stuff her mouth sometimes. If she had to hear one more time about "daddy this and daddy that," she would scream. Chrystal would cry late into the night afterwards. She missed her father to the extreme. Jackie wondered if it was even worth the effort to get Jimmy to spend time with his children.

Royce wasn't like Chrystal in that he didn't blame Jackie for the breakup. He took his father's desertion with little or no comments. He didn't act out in school, nor did he cry endlessly like Chrystal. Jackie wondered at the time how a nine, almost ten-year-old could be so quiet and stoic about the situation.

This was his father who didn't want to stay with the family anymore. The one man he should trust and looked to as a role model. The one man Royce truly loved, she thought. But Royce hunkered down and got into his books. He devoted all his time to science projects and things so technical that, half the time, she didn't even know what he was talking about.

His grandfather Buddy took over and guided little Royce as if he was his own son. Buddy taught him how to fish, how to take care of a car, how to be a man. God, how she wished Buddy was still here.

But all that paid off when Royce graduated from high school at sixteen. All the Ivy League schools courted him with full scholarships, but Jackie didn't want her baby to leave home. So she talked him into going to the most prestigious school in Atlanta and majoring in engineering.

At twenty, Royce had finished college early, had a wonderful girl who he met in college, and worked as an engineer with the power company. No, Royce wasn't perfect. Who can be? But he sure tried hard to do what was right. She guessed it was watching his sister go through one boy after the other and never finishing anything she started that gave him the incentive to do better.

Jackie did think that Royce and Jessica were probably rushing things a bit. They were both so young, and Jessica hadn't even finished college yet. Jackie hadn't gotten married until she was twenty-five and Jimmy was thirty, but she didn't want to think about that now. She knew how that story had ended. But as usual she couldn't help herself, and old memories could still hurt her deeply.

Looking back, maybe she should have paid more attention to Royce. But Chrystal was so needy and difficult to handle. At the time, she had believed she was doing what was best for both of her children. Besides, there was no one else she could go to for help for herself or anyone else, except a close friend at work, and she had about used them up. Her older sister, Nancy, had no children, had never been married or had any long-term relationships that Jackie knew of, for that matter.

Nancy had never liked Jimmy anyway. At first, Jackie thought Nancy was just jealous of her man, since she couldn't seem to get one. Nancy and Jimmy never could get along. Jimmy criticized Nancy and called her all kinds of ugly names, and Nancy returned the fire. She gave back just as good.

Nancy often said she didn't trust Jimmy. There was just something about him that didn't ring true. In fact, he seemed too good to be true. No one man could be that perfect. Jackie often found herself playing referee between the two. It got so bad that they stopped having Nancy over, and Jimmy made it plain that he really didn't want Jackie going over to Nancy's place either. Looking back, hindsight was twenty-twenty as they say. Maybe Nancy had the answer after all. Don't get yourself entangled with anyone, and you can't get hurt, and above all, never trust a man.

Jimmy's family was definitely out in terms of providing help too. They lived in Denver and didn't show much love for Jimmy and certainly not for her. Jimmy had a younger sister, Teresa, but he didn't seem to be close to her either. They were a strange family to say the least.

She also couldn't go to her parents. Buddy and Sylvia Stinson were the "until death do you part" kind of people. Her mother loved Jimmy. Jimmy always had a gift for her when they visited. Jackie remembered how Jimmy had even boasted that he and Ms. Sylvi made a better couple than he and Jackie. Ms. Sylvi would blush and stammer and make Jimmy's favorite pot roast, macaroni and cheese, and sweet potato pie for dessert. Jimmy could do no wrong in her eyes.

As far as issues with the kids, Ms. Sylvi didn't see any issues worth talking about. To her mother, the kids were fine. Royce was the star in Grandma Sylvi's eyes. Chrystal, well, Chrystal was spoiled and just needed a firmer hand. Even now, Jackie believed her mother thought the problems with her marriage lay with Jackie and not Jimmy. No one knew the real Jimmy or what had broken their marriage apart, but Jackie knew, and in her mind, no one else really needed to know.

Her father, Buddy, on the other hand would just stand to the side and shake his head. He always asked Jackie if Jimmy was treating her right. "You know you and the kids can always come home if that man is disrespecting you," he would say. It wasn't until later that the full meaning of her dad's words became clear.

When it all fell apart, it was her dad who stood beside her and told her that, no matter what, he would be there for her. Buddy had found her a lawyer when she came crying to her mom. Buddy had been the one who understood when she couldn't or wouldn't tell them what happened. It was Buddy, her wonderful father, who understood and found them a new house and even helped with the down payment. It was Buddy who opened the door for her, Chrystal, and Royce, and welcomed them home.

Again, how could she not have seen what was right in front of her eyes? It wasn't as if Jimmy was the type to confide in her about his feelings. That would have been too obvious. But there were signs aplenty.

Even before they were married, there were questions in her mind. He wasn't that eager to jump into bed with her for starters. In fact, she had to initiate the couplings most of the time. He would touch her so hesitantly, as if he didn't quite know what to do with her. She couldn't say it rocked her world, but it was okay. It would do. She thought with time it would get better and the intimacy she craved would come. Besides, he said he respected her too much to treat her like so many wild women in those days were acting. One-night affairs and booty calls were everywhere, and Jackie had made it plain she wanted more. She thought Jimmy wanted more also and they were sharing the same dream.

Their courtship didn't last long, and before she knew it, they were getting married. They had met in the spring, and by December they were married. In fact, it all happened so fast she sat back and let Jimmy handle everything. The wedding was small, just her family and a few close friends. Jimmy's sister, Teresa, was able to come but barely stayed long enough to congratulate the happy couple. It was as if she only came to verify that Jimmy was actually married and report back.

They honeymooned in the Bahamas, and on the first night Jimmy ate some bad conch and was sick for most of the week. He could barely lift his head from the pillow, so by no means could he do his husbandly duties. She ended up sitting alone on the beach or drowning her sorrows in gin and tonic in the hotel lobby bar. Certainly not the ideal situation, but she just knew things would get better once they got home.

After the honeymoon, even then she worked hard to get him in the mood. It took some doing. She wasn't a virgin and hadn't been since she was eighteen and first experimented with sex, but she wasn't an expert either. She looked to Jimmy to guide her, and unfortunately, it turned out she had to do the guiding.

He said it was the stress from his job, too much work to do at home, or his back was hurting. Hell, he wasn't but thirty-one, and his back had given out already? She didn't dispute him though. She tried to ease his pain with back rubs and long hot baths. He would fall asleep on her during the pampering and wake up the next morning as if everything had been wonderful the night before.

Sure, they had their moments. Every married couple had them. Jimmy was very stubborn about what he wanted to do or not. If she pushed too hard, he would completely withdraw from her, almost as if he was punishing her for wanting him. Jackie became so sexually frustrated she could cry. And she often did. Deep, gut-wrenching sobs when she was alone. She clutched a pillow to her face to muffle the sobs when Jimmy was at work or out of town, alternating between craving his touch and hating him to death. Her eyes would be red and burning by the time she reluctantly stopped. She had to do something; she couldn't go on this way.

Now, you flinch and laughingly wipe off my touch
As if my hand, my body, my soul were dirty
I am in withdrawal, aching for the yesterdays
When I hungered for your touch so mightily

Then finally, she was pregnant, and Jimmy all but heaved a huge sigh of relief. If their love-making was sketchy before, it was non-existent now. His parents came into town from Denver and oohed and aahed over little Chrystal when she was born, almost as if they were surprised Jimmy had produced such a beautiful baby. And Jimmy stood there and acted the proud daddy, when she, Jackie, had put everything on the line to make him a baby.

Then there was his friend, Bryan, who somehow was always in town or coming to town. Bryan, the "he always had my back and I would do anything for him" frat brother, was very good looking. He was from some little town in Louisiana, and he had café au lait skin, hazel eyes, and bright copper-colored hair. Jackie often wondered if the color was natural. Where Jimmy was tall and lean in all the right places, Bryan was the opposite. He was on the short side and had a slim build, almost soft. How she envied Bryan and the relationship he had with Jimmy. She decided she had to bust up their closeness, somehow.

Jackie tried several times to fix Bryan up with someone. First, there was Leslie from work. Leslie was a cute little thing and had a great personality, but their one and only date was a disaster. They had gone to the movies and later stopped at a local bar. Leslie said Bryan was so standoffish that he barely said a word all night. She ended up with a headache from drinking too much and trying so hard to find something interesting to say to him.

Bryan, on the other hand, said Leslie was okay, but she was nothing like Jackie. She just didn't compare. He needed someone like his frat brother had; no one else would do. At the time Jackie blushed, thinking it was a compliment.

Then, she tried her cousin Sheila. She and Sheila were running buddies and used to hit the clubs and dance all night when Jackie was going to college. Sheila was full of life and really just wanted to have a good time. Jackie set them up to go bowling. She thought maybe Sheila would bring Bryan out of his shell. She couldn't have been more wrong.

After their bowling date, Sheila told Jackie that Bryan was gay. Jackie didn't believe her and laughed it off. She told Sheila that Bryan was Jimmy's best friend and he would have said something if that was true.

Sheila said, "Well, whatever. My gaydar has never failed me yet. Maybe he's one of those who don't know it yet."

Bryan said everything had gone great and he had a fun time bowling. He even asked Jackie to set him up with Sheila again some time. He definitely wanted to stay in touch with her. But Jimmy took her to the side after that and told her to cool it with trying to set Bryan up. "Just let it be. Bryan's okay as he is."

Whenever Bryan was in town, which turned out to be too often, he always stayed with them. Jackie wondered if the man ever went to work. And of course Jimmy said he couldn't let his frat brother stay in a hotel. They had plenty of rooms in the big old Victorian. She never questioned the way they stayed up all night to reminisce. Jimmy would come to bed in the wee hours of the morning, more exhilarated and happier than ever. She didn't want to be a spoilsport. She never said no to anything they wanted to do together. But it wasn't as if Jimmy asked her beforehand; it was clear that this was what he would do and her opinion didn't matter.

Later, there were all the times he had to go to some conference for work and it just so happened that Bryan was also in the same town. Jimmy never wanted Jackie to go with him. Once, she went with him to Chicago, and Jimmy made her stay in the hotel room all day, waiting for him. It was one of the most boring trips of her life.

He only let her come to dinners his company had in town, like when he was accepting some award for one of his successful projects. On those occasions, he was so particular about what she would wear and how her hair was styled. Sometimes he went so far as to go shopping for her and come home with the outfit he wanted her to wear. He acted almost as if he was showing her off to his bosses. *Look at me I'm just one of the guys.*

He always made some excuse about why she should stay home if he needed to leave town. Even before the kids were born, Jimmy would say it was just too boring where he was going or he planned to hook up with his buddy Bryan and do guy stuff. Then after the kids came along, he changed his tune and said the kids may need her for some school activity or he wanted her home in case they got sick or something. He didn't trust daycare and babysitters to know what was best for his children. Her career was nothing compared to his, and he said she needed to be a mother first.

Jimmy's inattention to her when she talked about her wants and desires continued. To Jackie, it felt as if his mind was elsewhere when they made love, which was rare. He really wasn't into it. Now, in hindsight, it was so easy to see, but then, no one could have told her the truth.

Jimmy was always an immaculate dresser and very fastidious about his appearance. He stayed in the bathroom primping longer than she did. His semi-weekly appointments at the salon and his personal tailor were just some of the ways he lavished his money on himself. But Jackie liked the way he dressed and all those things about him that made him so special. Or so she thought until he started frowning at her about what she wore and how she did her hair, almost as if he was embarrassed to be seen with her. He would always ask the same old questions and try to tell her how to dress. *Why do you insist on dressing like a raggedy gypsy? You paint your fingernails such weird colors. Can't you tone it down some? Be more conservative in your wardrobe and hairstyle.*

Even before she decided to go natural and kept putting perm after perm into her hair to please him, he still complained. But afterwards he criticized her every time he looked her way. "You know the gas company is very conservative. How do you expect to advance, looking like that? You know you need to tame that lion. At least try to look more sophisticated and not so urban." He whined and complained every time they went anywhere together.

Everyone said they were made for each other; even their names went together, Jackie and Jimmy, what a pair. What the hell did "they" know?

She just knew it was another woman. There were too many whispered phone calls, and the "I'll be right back; just need to make a quick run" apologies. Yet, there were never any calls from other women that she knew of or jealous looks when they were out together. Could it be someone he worked with or some old college flame? The girls at Spelman were to die for. Every Morehouse man had a Spelman woman. Everybody knew that.

He never wanted her to come to his job either. He would always say, "Jackie, there's no reason for you to come all the way from Midtown to Alpharetta just to have lunch with me. The traffic is a killer. Besides, I usually work through lunch anyway. I'll just meet you somewhere closer to your job for dinner." Then he'd pat her on the head like she was his pet and go whistling on his way.

Maybe it was just her. Maybe she wasn't sexy enough or had gained too much weight with the birth of each child. She looked for any reason. But nothing fit, nothing seemed logical. Back then as she was experiencing it, she didn't want to believe it, didn't want to admit that she, Jackie Stinson, had made such a horrible mistake.

Jackie took several deep breathes after she heard the front door finally close and was sure Chrystal and the kids were gone. She went over to her desk in the corner of her bedroom. She took out the key she kept taped to the underside of the desk, opened the locked drawer, and took her laptop out. She turned it on and waited the few seconds it took to boot up. Carefully, she entered her password from the list she kept taped to its bottom. She often had trouble remembering the passwords since she changed them often, but she had come up with a system that worked. Being an analyst had its advantages. She would make up a short sentence about whatever was happening in her life at the time and turn it into an acronym.

Of all the secrets Jackie kept in her arsenal, her writing was the most dangerous and heavily guarded. She remembered what her best friend at work had told her years ago. *If you can't say it, try writing it down.* She did just that, but it was in the form of poetry and fictional short stories, not an actual diary. Her short stories were vehicles to hone her writing skills, but her poetry was how she truly felt. It contained every secret desire, every pain and heartache, every joy and happiness she had felt for the past twenty-five years. And it held the key to every love found and eventually lost.

She didn't have a laptop at first. She had a paper journal that she wrote in. Even then, she knew it was dangerous to write things down. She kept it well hidden in her bedroom of the small two-bedroom apartment she shared with a roommate, taped to the underside of her dresser drawers. It was more valuable to her than all her jewelry or money.

What if her roommate, Cheryl, found it and started reading? Jackie was so careful to never use real names, and sometimes the imagery sounded like one thing but actually masked something totally different. She had to be careful in case the journal fell into hostile hands.

After she was married, she was especially careful to never use names or places that someone could guess. Once she got a laptop, she converted all her colorfully written script into files on her computer. Jimmy being gone so much gave her the opportunity to get it all down, and she even wrote about his leaving her so often. In her silent house, she would write and then read them out loud. If it was especially heartfelt, the tears usually flowed and her throat would close up until she couldn't even read what she'd written.

I couldn't tell you calmly
I saved my breath, rushing to get it out
Yet you still never let me finish
You took command as always
General Know-It-All and damn the torpedoes

Now that I said it, you smile
Like you knew it before
The words even left my
Defeated lips that used to smile
Here I sit head down ready to apologize

Later when it was just her and the children, she would steal away to her room and start typing away. Royce was very bright and sometimes would hear her typing and ask what she was doing. "Just some work stuff, baby. Mama will be out in a little while," she answered. She never, never, never let anyone else read what she had written. Her family would be amazed, outraged, and scared to know just how good a writer she really was.

Okay, let's see, she thought. *I was writing about Royce and Jessica's wedding, but now I need to get this Chrystal mess down.* She started typing and the words flowed. It wasn't long before she had another masterpiece in the making.

Wednesday night – Chrystal's house

"Hey Smoke I don't know if I should have this stuff around the kids," whined Chrystal as she twisted her weave around and around her finger. "I don't want them to accidentally get into it." The cocky and smartass Chrystal was totally gone, and in her place stood an insecure woman-child who only wanted to be loved. Her mother would be amazed if she saw and heard this Chrystal.

"Girl, you worry too much. I got you. Didn't I tell you? Just do what I tell you, Chrystal, and leave the thinking to me. All them babies are asleep, and as long as you keep your cool, they'll stay that way and won't know nothing about this shit."

Smoke moved around Chrystal's place as if he owned it, or really like he owned Chrystal. Chrystal was so happy Chantrelle was over her mother's place. She didn't want anyone to see how Smoke treated and mistreated her. And to think she had stooped this low.

Smoke wasn't even cute with his old ass. He had to be at least thirty-five. And his real name is Calvin, she thought to herself. *With a name like Calvin, I would call myself something else too* and she wanted to laugh whenever she thought about it. Smoke had the biggest gut she had ever seen and big, popped eyes that protruded from their sockets. But worst of all, Smoke or Calvin, was an old, crusty, dusty-gray black, and he had the kinkiest, nastiest dreads this side of Decatur. She thought to herself, *he's so ugly he wouldn't make any kind of pretty babies.*

"Smoke, Nikki told me she was going to handle the stuff. You know I'm still on probation. I can't have this stuff in my house. Besides I told y'all I didn't want to have nothing to do with this side of the business. I just want to make the video like you said."

"You just shut your damn mouth and let me worry about this shit. I'm gonna put this shit way up here on the top shelf of this cabinet, way in the back. I'll come get it when I need it. Now, come here and take them pants off and give Smoke some of that sweet stuff."

Chrystal moved like a robot over to Smoke and did what he demanded; all the while, white hot tears dammed up in her eyes, ready to overflow. As she tried to blink them away, all she could think was what a shitty-ass way to live this was.

"Hey, Mom. You still up?" Royce turned from locking the door and setting the alarm to look at Jackie as he let himself in from the garage area. The kitchen was well lighted most times, but tonight all Jackie had on was some dim under-cabinet lighting. It barely picked up the sunny yellow the kitchen walls were painted. Jackie sat at the round café-style table in the center of the kitchen.

"Oh, hi, baby. I was just about to fix myself a little nightcap. Your sister and the kids left a little while ago. I guess I sort of lost track of time. How's Jessica? Better not be getting butterflies about the wedding." Jackie babbled on trying not to show her agitation.

Royce was a handsome young man, and to Jackie he looked just like his daddy. He got his conservative trait from Jimmy, she guessed. He always had on the latest fashions, but they were tasteful, button-down shirts and nice slacks, not baggy sweatshirts and loose jeans hanging off his ass. His eyes were the exact color of his dad's, a light brown, almost hazel, and his hair was brown, low cut, and wavy. *Yes*, she thought to herself, *the spitting image of his dad.*

"Mom, you know me. I wouldn't be getting married if I thought Jessica wasn't the one for me. And Jessica feels the same. We're ready to do this. I know you think we're both too young, but this is something I know is right."

"Okay, I know you're right. I just have to ask. I don't want you to feel pressured. Your engagement wasn't that long, and Jessica is still in school—"

"Mom, don't worry about me and Jessica. We're cool. Besides, what was big sis doing here at this time of night? I know you didn't give her any more money. I love my sis, but she goes through money like water. Those kids have to be the most fashionably dressed toddlers in the world. What with all the junk she buys. And you don't help any with all the stuff you get them."

Jackie threw up her hands and said, "Guilty. I know I buy way too many toys and clothes, but I want the kids to feel loved and look nice. I don't want my grandbabies to look like hood rats. Besides, she didn't come looking for money this time. Chrystal wanted me to keep the kids while she went to Miami to shoot a video with some guy named Smoke."

"What? You have got to be kidding me. I know Chrystal is crazy, but not even she would come out this time of night and ask you something stupid like that. Please tell me you didn't agree to do it."

Jackie moved around the kitchen, making herself some tea. "No, Royce. I told her I couldn't do that with everything going on with the wedding and all, and she about had a fit. She just cussed me out too. Said I had never done anything for her and accused me of doing too much for you. All the while, them little babies were crying and hollering. All it did was dig up old mess, and now my head is aching terribly."

"Do you think Chrystal is back on the stuff? I know she promised she would stay clean if you helped her with all that mess that went down. You'd think she had learned her lesson. And who in the world is Smoke?"

Jackie shook her head and slowly answered as Royce took a seat at the table. "I wish I knew, but you know how she is. She never gives you enough information to really know anything. She did say he was some sort of record producer or something and they were making this video in Miami."

Jackie took a sip of her tea and said, "Finally, after we had fought like cats and dogs, she calmly tells me that the shoot is off and Smoke is coming to get them. She told me not to worry about her and her kids. Her new man was going to take care of them."

"I think I might have heard about a guy named Smoke that's supposed to be some big-time producer. But I have no idea how Chrystal would have gotten connected to him. Chrystal does do what Chrystal wants though. She practically lives on Facebook and Snapchat, so who knows? She always manages to find a way. Three kids haven't slowed her down in the least. But promise me, Mom that you won't let her get to you like that. It's all just emotional blackmail. You have nothing to be guilty about. You've done everything you could to help. I think you've probably done too much. Chrystal is so selfish. I wish sometimes that—"

"No, Royce. Don't feel that way about your sister. I pray for you and her constantly. You know I love you all more than anything, and I wouldn't know what to do with myself if something happened to either of you. Besides, you know I'm not in any condition to take care of three little Chrystals," said Jackie with a smile as she pushed her chair back from the table to get up. "Their mama is about all I can stand, and I can't stand that."

"Okay, Mom. I think I'm going to call it a night. I got a bunch of running around to do tomorrow. You should be getting to bed too. Get that beauty sleep, not that you need it."

"Good night, baby, and you better behave tomorrow. Only a few more days, and you'll be a married man. Don't let me tell Jessica on you," said Jackie, laughing as she hugged Royce.

Jackie fixed herself another cup of herbal tea. She needed something stronger like a gin and tonic, but she had to get up early in the morning to go to work. Herbal tea and a couple of Excedrin tension tablets would have to do. She knew if she lived to be a hundred, she would never understand her daughter, but if God was willing, she would keep on trying and keep on giving her children love.

 **3**

What's the color of your tears?
Brazen blues that lie and distort
Cowardly corals to highlight your fears
Envious emerald full of shame and remorse

Jackie had finally gotten into bed. She tossed and turned, reliving the night's events. She didn't know what to do with Chrystal and hated that she even had to think about. *If Jimmy had never come into my life*, she thought; but that was wrong. You can't undo the past and she really did love Chrystal. Didn't she?

Jackie didn't want to think about her ex, Jimmy, but it seemed he always came up in her mind these days. She remembered some old folks saying that if you kept thinking about somebody, they were somewhere talking about you. She didn't want to think Jimmy was somewhere talking about her. She didn't want Jimmy to even think about her, much less speak her name. *Crazy*, she thought. *I don't want to think about him.* But she couldn't help but think back to how it all began.

Over twenty-five years ago

Fresh out of Georgia State College with high ideals and a business degree, Jackie felt on top of the world. She had managed to get a job as assistant to the department head for the Bureau of Parks, and for the 1980s, she pulled in a good salary to boot. However, she had no idea the political wrangling that drove those types of positions, and soon disillusionment replaced her high ideals. After a couple of years, she was going nowhere with the city government.

Her friend Leslie told Jackie about openings at the gas company, where she worked, and after three interviews and more tests than she'd taken in college, Jackie was hired as an administrative assistant to a mid-level manager. Times were changing so fast that a college degree didn't get you to the same places in life anymore, so she took advantage of every educational opportunity that came up in her company. She embraced any opportunity to get herself ready for the next great thing; because "you can never be too prepared" was her motto and words she lived by. Soon she was rising faster and further than she had ever dared hope, and then James "Jimmy" Mattock came into her life.

She met James Mattock on the job. She and the rest of her department were attending a company presentation on new and emerging technologies in the gas industry. It was spring in Atlanta, and instead of paying attention to the moderator announcing the next speaker, she was looking out the window at the fresh spring blossoms. *They should have known better than to have windows in these conference rooms, with all that sunny springtime-ness going on outside*, she thought. At that moment, something other than the bird in the tree outside caught her attention. There was a new speaker at the podium, and he was really something else.

Jackie leaned over to her friend Leslie and asked, "I didn't get his name. Who is that up there?"

Leslie chuckled and said, "Girl, you should've been paying attention. He's a big-shot manager with Rayex Industries. They say he knows everything about computer-generated gas exploration. He's really cute isn't he? His name is James something."

Jackie tried to take this new speaker's measure in one long glance. He was tall, at least six-two. He had on a nicely tailored blue suit, and a beautiful red tie complemented his blue-and-white striped shirt. His face was what you would call "handsome on anybody," what with the small mustache he was sporting. He had a medium-brown complexion and a slightly sharp nose. Nice, low, wavy haircut. He looked to be in his late twenties. And man, he was runway model perfect. Now this was better than the view out the window.

Jackie tried to compare him to her current boyfriend, Larry Woodard, and poor Larry came up woefully inadequate to say the least. Larry was barely taller than her, and he was not a dresser. Besides, Larry was an auto mechanic, which in itself was a great blue-collar job, but this man was at least a department head in computer technology. He had to be making a lot of money. She could tell by how his suit fit him perfectly. It wasn't that she was a snob; it was just a matter of weighing one's options. She wanted the most she could get out of life and it looked as if this man could do that for her.

Whoa there, girl. You don't even know this man, and already you're thinking about him as yours. She listened to his speech a little longer, trying to get back to the topic at hand. Suddenly, he concluded and asked if there were any questions.

Jackie looked around the room, waiting for someone to ask a question, just to keep this Adonis up there longer. A few hands went into the air, so Jackie tried to listen to what he was saying so she could get his voice down with the look. A few suck-ups asked about opportunities in computer technology as it pertained to gas explorations, but Jackie knew she was in love. It wasn't just his look or his voice, it was just him.

The room broke up around her, and Leslie nudged Jackie to get her attention. "Jackie! Girl, wake up. You look like you been drinking or something. Your eyes are all glazed over and everything. Why are you looking at that man like that? Do you know him or something?"

Everyone was standing up around her, and she stood up also. "No, I don't know him yet, but I will before this day is over." She couldn't believe those bold words came from her mouth. She had never been this aggressive towards anyone in her life. What was happening here? She had a boyfriend, and she was practically engaged. *Yeah, but not to this man,* a nagging little voice shot back.

"Leslie, I'll meet you back at the office. I'm just going to hang around and see if there's anything else Mr. James might need."

"Okay, all right, I guess I'll see you for lunch," Leslie said as she backed away. "I've never seen you act this way about anyone before. I hope you're not moving too fast. Jackie do you hear me?" Jackie totally ignored her friend as Leslie turned away shaking her head.

Jackie managed to look as if she was just gathering her belongings as she felt eyes on her. She looked up and made eye contact with James what's-his-name, still at the podium gathering up his stuff.

"You look like you're having a little trouble getting your gear together. Need some help? I don't have to be back at my office for a while." James delivered this little speech with a bright smile.

"Yeah, I could use a little help. I think my purse strap got stuck in the back of the chair somehow."

Jackie watched as James casually came over to her seat and expertly detangled her purse strap from the folding chair. He was even better looking up close. His cologne was dynamite also. She thought it was that new Calvin Klein fragrance, and it was subtle, not too overpowering, just like the man wearing it. She was suddenly a little nervous. She had never reacted this quickly and strongly to anyone else before, and she didn't know why she was feeling the way she was.

"Hi. My name is Jackie Stinson. I work in human resources. I didn't catch your entire name. Your first name is James, isn't it?"

"Yes, James Mattock, at your service. My friends call me Jimmy, and I think you'll be one of my friends. How about we get a cup of coffee before the cafeteria closes? Talking always dries out my throat, and I feel like having a little drink with you will restore me to my full potential." He gave her a wink with his dark brown, almost black eyes fringed with the longest lashes she had ever seen on a man.

"Why James, uh Jimmy, I would love a cup of coffee. I think we're going to be great friends also. I have a little time before I have to be back at my desk. What better way to spend it than finding out about all the latest emerging technologies the gas company's involved in?" Jackie couldn't believe this gorgeous man was flirting with her and, yes, she was flirting back. That cup of coffee turned into dinner later on that night.

Jackie loved everything about Jimmy Mattock. One dinner turned into more dinners and then breakfasts and then all-nighters. She was an Atlanta native but had never been to the places Jimmy took her: the restaurants he frequented in the most upscale locations, the art museum, and the high-end boutiques. He opened up a world for her that she didn't even know existed. He was so special, and he treated her so respectfully.

It was the late eighties, and she was young and out to get hers. But somewhere in the back of her mind, she did wonder if maybe she was moving too fast—and was Jimmy really all that? But if she wanted to live the 'good life' she knew this was the path to it.

Jackie wasted no time getting rid of her boyfriend, Larry Woodard. Every time poor Larry called, she told her roommate, Cheryl, to say she was out. After two weeks, she broke it off completely with the "It's me, not you" excuse and "I'm not ready to settle down yet." She knew Larry was hurt, but what the hell, she was in love for the first time in her life and Larry be damned.

Cheryl cautioned her to take it slow. "Girl that dude is fine, but he's a little older and there's just something about him. I can't put my finger on it. I just don't want you to get hurt."

"I know, Cheryl, but Jimmy is so much more than I ever thought I could get. Yeah, I know he's five years older, but that just means he's more mature and ready to settle down. I can see us having babies together."

Cheryl went on defending Larry. "Larry is just so kind, and yeah I know, kind of simple, but he's sweet, and he treats you like a queen. All the free tune-ups, tires, and engine overhauls you can stand."

"But, girl," Jackie said, "Jimmy has a fantastic job, and he already has his own house, and he drives some kind of fine car and just ... Just everything about him is so great. For the first time in my life, I'm happy and I think—nah, I know—I'm in love. You know he went to Morehouse, and he's so intelligent and dresses so sharp. I just feel it's right."

"I understand, but it's only been a few weeks, and already you're sleeping over his place, and poor Larry. I just don't want you to wake up and it's all a nightmare. But I will say this. If he really is the one, ask him if he's got a brother or cousin or a friend 'cause I sure could use one of him too."

Jackie laughed along with Cheryl at her joke, but Cheryl's questioning did make Jackie a little nervous. Yes, she had stayed over at Jimmy's house, but it was so platonic that even Jackie wondered. He gave her some really good kisses. But it never went any further than that, and he didn't even initiate those. She had to practically throw herself into his arms to get him to kiss her. Even though she had clearly indicated she was ready to take it to the next level, Jimmy always had a reason to keep things as they were.

"Jackie, baby," he would say in that smooth baritone of his, "I have too much respect for you to use you that way. We'll both know when it's the right time. Until then, let's just take things as they come." This answer usually made Jackie a little ashamed of herself. Was she that much of a whore that she couldn't wait to jump this man's bones? If she was honest with herself, the answer was probably yes.

"Hey Jackie, you're home early. Why don't you come and get into bed? You look beat," said a smugly smiling Jimmy as Jackie opened the bedroom door and came into the room.

"Sure, honey. I'm so tired." As Jackie neared the bed, she saw the spot a naked Jimmy was patting. But more clearly, she saw a naked Bryan scooting over and grinning to make room for her. All she could do was scream.

Thursday morning – present day

Jackie woke up and struggled to get up out of bed. She'd just had the same old nightmare. Even though it happened more than ten years ago; it always left her twisted up in her sticky, sweaty nightgown. She gave up and flopped back down deeper into the soft mattress. According to the bedside alarm clock, it was 8:30 in the morning already. The sun was trying to light up the room through her dark-lined, violet-colored drapery, but even it couldn't penetrate the gloom. She liked it this way; it mirrored how she usually felt inside.

Like the nightmare that wouldn't end, all she saw in her mind's eye was the day she came home early, sick and exhausted, and heard strange noises coming from upstairs. She quietly eased up the stairs.

What a fool she'd been. If it had been a gunman waiting to blow her head off, she wouldn't have been more dumbfounded. As she crept to the partially open bedroom door, all she saw was Jimmy's naked ass on top of an equally naked Bryan, and they both were moaning and groaning.

The old nightmare didn't come close to what really happened though. She hadn't screamed; in fact, she hadn't said a word at first. She'd just picked up the closest thing to her hand, which happened to be the hideously carved wooden statue that Bryan had given them as a wedding gift. It was tall and had a good weight to it, just right to use as a weapon. Jimmy and Bryan didn't hear or see her until she was almost on top of them. Just as she raised the statute to beat the shit out of Jimmy, Bryan, who lay on his stomach must have seen her out of the corner of his eye.

"Oh my God, Jackie! What are you doing here?" Bryan screeched. He bolted up, struggled to get Jimmy off him, and tried to cover his nakedness with the sheet all at the same time. Jimmy calmly, much too calmly, rolled over and looked at Jackie.

"I suppose you want an explanation," Jimmy said as he rolled his eyes toward Bryan and snatched the sheet off him. "Get up, Bryan, and go into the bathroom and take a shower. I need to talk to Jackie alone."

Jackie couldn't even think straight. Her tears fell like a black monsoon. It wasn't that she was so surprised. No, she was absolutely furious. She slowly lowered the statute and watched Bryan as he rushed into the bathroom and closed the door behind him. And the nerve of that little slut with his juicy ass, he even locked the door. If looks could kill, both Jimmy and Bryan would be six feet deep, stacked one on top of the other.

The thought almost made her smile, but instead she spoke softly so Jimmy had to sit up to hear her. "You're just a sorry-ass, worthless, piece of common shit! Right here in my own damn bed. And to think I gave you everything I had as a woman, and you needed to fuck a man, or whatever." She pointed a shaking finger towards the closed bathroom door.

"I had babies for you. I put my career on the back burner for you, and I put up with your stupid family and friends for you, you down-low piece of slime! You bring your lover, your frat brother, you said; you bring him into my home and fuck him in my bed! I gave you everything I had to give as your wife, and this is how you repay me?"

Jimmy just looked at her.

Jackie's voice trembled as she continued. "I rubbed your damn back for you and listened to you whine and carry on about how I looked and dressed. Fifteen years I put up with your sensitive ass and all your bullshit. If I made two cents, you took one and a half. 'For our future,' you said. I never said anything about what you did or didn't do. I let you make every decision about the house, the children, everything. I was so stupid I thought you loved me."

Jimmy slowly sat up and swung his legs off the side of the bed. He gave Jackie a disgusted look. "Jackie," he said, "put that statute down, and sit your ass down."

Without realizing it, Jackie moved even closer to the bed. "I tried to change myself into whatever you told me to be because I loved you, and all the while, you didn't want my pussy because you wanted some dick!" Her eyes were so blinded with scalding, red-hot tears she didn't realize Jimmy had gotten up and was wrapping the sheet around him until he pulled the statute out of her hands.

"Are you finished with your pity party?" Jimmy took the statue, put it back up on the dresser, and casually sat down in the armchair beside the bed. "If so, maybe I can get a word in."

"I know you didn't just sit your black ass in that chair like you and Bryan had just been out playing basketball or something. I walk in here and just about throw up because you got your dick shoved up some guy's ass, and you ask me am I just about finished talking?"

Jackie took a few steps back and shook her head. "You must believe I'm the craziest woman in the world if you think I want to listen to anything you got to say. If I had a gun right now, I'd blow your shitty balls right off." Jackie was so angry all she could do was wheeze and shake. She hugged her arms around herself and let her ashen tears fall.

Jimmy answered with indignation. "Well, first, this is my house and this is my bed. I bought and paid for them, just like I bought and paid for you. I will fuck whoever I please in my bed, and let me add that Bryan is a much better fuck than you ever were or could be!"

Jimmy crossed his legs and draped the sheet around him as if it were a toga. "Furthermore, if I had known you'd be this much trouble, I would have left your nappy-headed ass sitting in that damn chair all those years ago."

Jackie stared at Jimmy as if seeing him for the first time. Were her ears functioning? She couldn't have heard him correctly. "What the hell did you just say?" she finally managed to stammer out, as she wiped snot and tears off her face.

"I said—and listen carefully this time—if I'd known you would be this much trouble, I would have left your ass in that conference room years ago. I've tried my damn best to make you into the woman I needed. You were intelligent, not ugly, seemed to have your head on straight. But I underestimated the degree of your selfishness. I thought you'd be malleable enough to fit into my plans for accomplishing my goals."

Jackie looked at Jimmy as if he had three heads and six mouths. This couldn't be the man she married and thought she loved. She knew he was sort of ruthless when it came to his work, but to have planned exactly how he would use her? And use her was exactly what he'd done since the beginning. Jimmy had never been the romantic type, spouting pretty poetry but this person sitting here was so cold and calculating that he could look her in the eyes and say the things he was saying. And he'd probably planned this whole scene too. He wanted her to catch him. He wanted to be found out. She had called his cell phone and left a message, telling him she was sick and going home to rest. Now he was sitting there with a wet dick he just pulled out of his lover's ass! What kind of hellish maniac had she lain down with?

"You mean to tell me that I was just a fucking means to an end? Just a front for you to look legitimate. I just don't understand. I don't want to understand." Jackie shook her head over and over again. She knew she must be hallucinating, or this had to be some horrible elaborate prank. This could not be happening to her. She could not have been that foolish. She could not have been that blind.

She continued with big shuddering breaths. "Are you saying you ... you never loved me? You never cared about me? Your children, Chrystal and Royce, you don't love them? That this, this is the real you, and everything else is just a big fat lie? Did I just imagine everything we had together? Did you plan this whole thing, to let me catch you like this? Was I the biggest fool, that stupid, oh my God . . . ?"

She could barely get the words out clearly before she was left completely speechless. She hung her head as far as it would go, her chin resting on her chest. Rivers of violet tears ran down her indigo blouse, leaving a lavender trail. Her arms flopped at her sides, useless. Her fists were balled so tightly that her fingernails cut into her palms, leaving crescent-shaped imprints. She was dead from the top of her head to the tips of her toes. It was as if someone had hammered a huge nail into the center of her body, her very heart, and let all her scarlet life-blood out.

Jimmy made a sound half way between a laugh and a snort. "Don't be ridiculous. I didn't plan this, and I have grown to care for you all in my own way. I'm not the monster you're trying so fucking hard to paint. Bryan and I have been together since college. He knows me like no other, and I have very deep feelings for him. I am just who I am. And I'm not going to apologize for that, not ever.

"In fact, I've never actually portrayed myself to be anything other than what I am. I can't help it if you chose to believe something different. I gave you time to understand, but you never seemed to accept it. I never offered you love and fidelity or the perfect marriage. If you remember, I asked you to be my wife, to help me in my business dealings, and to maintain a household with me. You wanted something different, something more.

"Like I said, I underestimated your damn selfishness and stubbornness. I didn't think you wanted babies, but I did what I needed to do to give you that. Now that they're here, I care for them too. Besides, I never asked you about your activities while I was out of town. I definitely know you didn't just sit here waiting for me like a love-sick, neglected wife. I know you had plenty of company. I have my friends at the gas company too." Jimmy said all this as if it was perfectly logical. As if any fool could understand the rationality of his plans.

Jackie felt all the air leave her lungs with each biting word from her husband's mouth. Her knees weakened and her hands shook uncontrollably. She felt something like pinpricks all over her body, burning and stinging. Bile rose in her throat, and she felt she would choke on the horrible, horrible truth. She tried to block out his words, in fact she didn't even hear most of what he said about her friends. She only knew he had betrayed her in the worst possible way.

For without a doubt, this was the real Jimmy Mattock, and this was how it really was. This betrayal was so much worst, so much more than she had ever imagined. It was more than she could take in.

The fact that Jimmy was gay, she understood. Well, sort of. She had suspected for some time. Even that he and Bryan were involved didn't completely surprise her because they were just too damn close to only be frat brothers. That he wanted someone else, she could fight against. She could deal with that reality to a certain degree. But to use her in this way, as he had, and for so long, with no regard to her as a human being, that shredded her soul to ribbons. She was just another tool to him to be used and discarded.

Jackie suddenly grabbed a big handful of her hair and tugged and pulled on it. She needed to distract herself somehow. So many thoughts ran through her head that she felt dizzy, and she knew that if she didn't get out of that room, that house, she would hurt somebody really, really badly. She thought about who she had given up and at what cost. All because she thought Jimmy loved and needed her. She had thrown away the only good man in her life, and for what? A lying, manipulative, gay bastard! She wanted to hurt Jimmy so badly. To somehow make him pay for all the years she had wasted trying to make this marriage work.

"Jackie, sit down, and let's discuss this. The kids will be home soon from school, and I don't want them to find us all like this." Jimmy looked nervously towards the bathroom, spreading his hands out to encompass them all.

Jackie saw movement near the bathroom and saw that Bryan had opened the door to peek out; probably looking for his clothes he left on the bench. *He dresses just the way Jimmy wants me to.* She almost giggled hysterically at the irony.

"You know what?" she said. "I don't want to sit down. I don't want to discuss anything with the two of you. You and Bryan can just go back to fucking each other. You know you're good at that because you sure have fucked me over royally. I don't care if the kids will be home soon. You should have thought about that before you started getting your little dick assed up. I'm leaving. You can tell them whatever the hell you want. I just don't give a damn anymore!"

Jackie stumbled her way out of the bedroom. She was so blinded by tears she could barely see the stairs to make her way down.

"Jackie, wait. Don't leave like this. You'll just hurt yourself," Jimmy said as he made a move towards the stairs still wearing his improvised toga. Bryan had wrapped a towel around his waist and slowly followed him.

"What the hell do you care?" she threw the words back over her shoulder. "Remember I'm just a means to an end. I'm too damn stubborn to control. Too selfish to just do what I'm told and turn a blind eye to all this shit. I couldn't see what was right in front of my face. No, don't worry about me. I will be … all right." Her voice broke on a choking sob so heartbreakingly wretched that even Bryan shed a tear.

I used to believe in your magic
It lifted me higher and made my steps so light
You branded me with your touch upon my soul
I knew the entire world turned upon your command
I was helpless and didn't want to understand differently

Now the very air from your lips stings and
Bites with an artic frostiness that freezes
Turning my crimson blood a muddy gray
My used-to-be-warm, flowing blood that
Sprung from my heart that truly loved you

Jackie found her purse, banged through the kitchen door, leaving it open as she went into the garage. She jammed the key into the ignition of her BMW and raced out of the garage with barely enough room for the car to get under the rising door. As the car sped down the street, scarcely under control, she shuddered and sighed as each shimmering tear fell unhindered.

❧

She came back after a few days. It was the weekend, and the kids raced to her side when she came through the door. "Mama, I missed you so much. Daddy said you had to go and take care of Grandma Sylvi for a few days. Is she okay?" Chrystal hugged Jackie tight before she let go.

"Did he now? Yes, baby, Grandma is all right. She sends her love to both of you. I love you both so much, and I've missed you guys like crazy. Has Daddy been taking good care of you both?"

Jackie patted both their heads and hugged Royce to her.

He gave her a gentle squeeze in return and said," I love you, Mom."

Just then Jimmy came into the kitchen, got a beer out of the refrigerator, and leaned on the counter. He gave her a look that dared her to say more.

"Yes, Mom," said Royce, "but Dad doesn't cook as good as you. My stomach is still empty, and he took us to IHOP for breakfast. It was good, but your pancakes are better."

"Well, I tell you what. How about we take a little trip, just the three of us? Daddy has to work and can't join us. We can go to Disney World. How does that sound?"

"Mama, are you for real? I'm ready right now," squealed Chrystal. "I'm going upstairs to pack. Man, no school next week! Yay!"

"Me too," Royce answered as he raced after his sister.

Jackie turned slowly back to Jimmy, who still leaned on the counter. So far, he hadn't said a word, only stared her down. Jackie picked up her purse and turned to go upstairs.

"Hold on. I need to talk to you," said Jimmy as he roughly grabbed her by the arm. "Just what do you think you're doing? You walk out of here as if you don't have a care in the world and you're gone for three days with God only knows who. You don't call, no messages, nothing. Now you come in here and tell my kids you're taking them to Disney World. We have things we need to talk about."

Jackie just as roughly knocked Jimmy's hand off her arm. "No, Jimmy, I don't have anything left to say to you. I don't owe you any explanations as to where I've been. I'm going upstairs to pack all my hideous clothes you can't stand, all my ugly hair products, anything that belongs to me and only me, and then I'm going to make sure the kids have all their stuff they need out of this unholy house."

"Wait a minute. Do you really think I'm going—"

"I don't give a fuck what you're going to do! I couldn't care less what you want. I'm taking the kids to Disney World with your money, and when we get back, I'm going to my parents' house with them. If there's anything I want or need that's left in this house of horrors, I'll send my father over to get it. I'll let you know when he'll be coming, so you can vacate the premises. If you don't like it, then tough shit because I'm through with being used by you."

She cried all the way upstairs, sweating so badly the space between her breasts was slick and soaked through to the front of her blouse. This was one of the hardest things she'd ever had to do. As she walked away, she could feel Jimmy's eyes boring into her back. His hate was a real, living beast that followed her all the way out of the house.

Thursday morning – present day

Jackie looked around her dim bedroom. She saw all the furniture she had so lovingly picked out to furnish this room. It was totally different from the bedroom she had shared with Jimmy. She loved shabby chic and flea market finds. Jimmy favored old world antiques. Unfortunately this room saw about as much action as the one she had with Jimmy. She gave herself a moment to remember the last time she had been in the old Victorian. The divorce court had said half of everything was hers but she hadn't wanted a thing except her personal items.

She had left everything else in the house with Jimmy when she left. After all, it was his stuff from the beginning, and she especially didn't want the Regency king-sized bed she and Jimmy and Jimmy and Brian had shared.

Jimmy had always bought everything for the house, and he never consulted her on the purchases beforehand. In a lot of ways, she'd felt like an unwanted guest in her own home. Jimmy's house in Midtown didn't have one iota of her taste in it. The few personal items she did take and the children's things all fit nicely in the new home her father helped them find. She bought new and some old bedroom furniture and, over time, living and dining room furniture also. It may have been a little bohemian, but she liked it.

But here she was, at forty-nine, with grown-ass children, a grandmother no less, and what did she have to show for it? A failed marriage with a down-low piece of shit. It was a miracle he hadn't given her some incurable disease.

She had her children of course. Royce was everything a mother could want in a son. He was smart and good-looking, and so far had shown no gay tendencies that she knew of. Chrystal was ... was what? Chrystal, Jackie couldn't understand. Her daughter was a beautiful woman, but she acted as if she had no respect for herself. As if, somehow, she was less deserving of real love, and of course, she looked for what love she settled for in all the wrong people. What had Jackie and Jimmy done to Chrystal to make her this way?

Jackie couldn't help but think about the conversation she'd had with Jimmy about their daughter. She had reached out to him when Chrystal was pregnant the first time. Jackie had needed to swallow every bit of her pride to call him in the first place, and he had said the worst things she could have imagined. He'd barely acknowledged her polite hello and inquiry about how he was doing before he cut her off.

"Just tell me what you want," was all he said.

She told him the situation they were in, begged him to at least talk to Chrystal so they could find out who the father was and take some sort of legal action if necessary. She asked him if he could help with some of the expenses, just lend a helping hand. She was glad later that Chrystal wasn't there to hear the conversation.

"I guess you want me and Bryan to supply more child support, huh? Well I'm sure as hell not going to do it. I'm not even sure Chrystal is my child, but now you want me to send money for her baby too! I knew I should have gotten a paternity test on her and Royce too. They look nothing like me. I may be gay, but you're one black, crazy-ass bitch if you think I'm going to send one penny for Chrystal's little bastard. You made this mess. Now you fix it!"

Hurt like she'd never known filled her heart. *Damn his bitch-ass soul to hell.* Where had her mind been? Through it all, she never thought he knew. When had he started suspecting her? Oh Lord, if he had told Chrystal and Royce, she couldn't stand the thought. The guilt overwhelmed her, and it was a heavy burden to bear.

It hadn't started out that way. When she was pregnant the first time, Jimmy wasn't around much as her pregnancy advanced, but when she delivered, he was right there holding her hand. When Chrystal was born, his eyes lit up like Fourth of July fireworks. He couldn't get enough of their daughter. He would hold her as if she was the most precious gift he had ever been given. And Jackie was so proud, so happy that she'd been able to give him a baby. Although it wasn't the son she thought every man wanted first, Chrystal was a beautiful baby. She had a head full of dark, glossy curls, more hair than Jackie thought a baby should have, and her eyes, once they opened completely, were such a delicate light brown that they sparkled.

"I wonder which side of the family she got those eyes from," Jimmy had said as he tried to catch on to Chrystal's little flailing hands. "I remember my grandmother having eyes like that, but I didn't think it would skip two generations."

Jackie had cleared her throat and said, "Yes I didn't think so either, but apparently it can. She looks just like your mom though. Look at those ears. And her hair is just like yours. We got us the most beautiful baby in the world."

Jimmy was never more attentive to her than in those few months after Chrystal was born. But as the years went by, he paid less and less attention to Chrystal. And Jackie didn't think it was possible, but Chrystal picked up on it. He didn't hold her as much or take her with him when he went out. The kisses to her curly hair and "let me hold Daddy's little princess" stopped. And then he went right back to out of town trips and "busy with work stuff." He was much too busy for them. Jackie had thought she had to do something.

And when Royce came along, Jimmy completely forgot about Chrystal. Jackie remembered a little four-year-old Chrystal looking at her as she fed a curly-haired Royce. "Daddy loves him more. He don't even piggy-back ride me no more," Chrystal had said, crying big, golden teardrops while sucking on her fingers. Jackie's heart had broken because she knew it was true.

Maybe Chrystal was the way she was because she had been conceived in desperation. Jackie would and did do anything to give Jimmy a baby. She believed this was the reason for Jimmy's inattention and neglect. But Chrystal was so fussy as a baby that only Jimmy could handle her. She cried for attention, food, and diaper changes, whatever she felt she didn't have at the time from Jimmy. Every time Jackie tried to intervene Chrystal would scream louder until Jimmy took her in his arms. If Jackie tried to feed her she would spit it out and a rainfall of blue tears would ensue. All Jimmy had to do was coo at her and she would open her mouth wide and gobble it all down. At bedtime Jackie had to fight a struggling Chrystal to calm down whereas Jimmy only had to pick her up and she would quiet and sleep peacefully all night long. The daytime hours became a hell whenever Jimmy wasn't around.

Was Chrystal this way because Jackie had wanted so badly to have a baby, thinking it would take away all the troubles in her marriage? Had Chrystal felt the desperation even in the womb? She had done everything in her power to make a baby. And she was successful.

Royce, on the other hand, was conceived in joy and love. Royce was her good baby. He was always calm and patient, waiting eagerly for his food with a big toothless smile. She could make a simple silly face and he would giggle and coo. She had never been in a better place in her life than when she carried Royce. It brought Jimmy back home, and he rubbed her back and stomach for her. He did everything he could to live up to his vows. Bryan still came into town, but Jimmy didn't run off with him as much. Everything was finally right in her world. She was so happy then.

What's the color of your tears?
Dry heaves of eyes instead of guts
Angry scarlet waterworks of fears
Diminished only by barren ducts

Friday morning – a day before the wedding

Jackie stretched and looked at the clock. Nine-thirty in the morning. She had time. Her appointment at the nail salon wasn't until 11:30, so why not take advantage of a day off to sleep in? It had been a little hard to get to sleep last night. What with her hot flashes and having to get up several times during the night to change her nightgown and turn up the air conditioner, she was more than a little worn out. And Royce would probably go into shock and have a complex if he saw his mother naked. So night after night, she endured the torture of the gowns.

She wanted to sleep in the nude, but with the way her body clung to the extra weight these days, she was too embarrassed. Her mind told her that the paramedics would laugh at the sight of her if they had to break into her house for an emergency. She didn't want to get caught butt naked with everything hanging out.

It wasn't like a lot of hot, heavy love making went on. Her bedroom had become her retreat, a place to get centered. Where her inner-most thoughts and emotions got a chance to come out and play. But as usual she remembered the past and her less than successful attempts at dating.

Ten years ago

Much later, once the initial shock of Jimmy's betrayal had lessened, she had dated some, but all the men seemed to have something wrong with them. Not that she was a Halle Berry or something, but shit, she wasn't that bad.

She had to laugh to herself about one guy in particular, who a crazy-ass co-worker fixed her up with for dinner. She should have known better than to trust Gary. She could hardly work with him without him getting on her nerves, and she knew he didn't have good sense or taste. But Gary kept begging her to give his friend a chance.

Well, that man came to her house and asked for money because, he said, he didn't have enough cash on him to pay the cab driver waiting outside. Jackie told him all she had was a dollar and he could go on and catch a bus back to wherever. He managed to find the cab fare after all. He must have thought she was some kind of stupid.

Talk about sorry, and then he asked her what she had cooked for dinner because he sure was hungry. Not to mention the guy looked like a cross between Yoda and a big fat frog. Ugh! She told him she hadn't cooked anything because she thought they were going out to eat. He ended up walking down the street to the bus stop.

What was that guy's name? Yeah, Jerry Daniels or something, and he left mad too, like he was the one who had the lousy date.

She sat up in bed and shook her head at the memory. When she saw Gary at work, she chewed him out good. He swore he didn't know his friend was that broke. "But you knew he was that ugly, and you could have warned a girl," Jackie had told him.

And then there was the deacon at the church her mother attended. Ms. Sylvi had told Jackie that all the best men went to church. Jackie had laughed and said, "Well, Ma, just because you met daddy at church a hundred years ago don't mean lighting will strike like that for me."

But she was willing to give it a try, so when Deacon Connelly asked her if he could escort her to the church picnic, she accepted. Little did she know that a fifty-five-year-old, balding, chubby church deacon would have the moves of an eighteen-year-old boy. From the minute he picked her up in his Chevrolet, it was hands on. His hands on her body, that is. That man tried to stick his sweaty hands everywhere, and he hadn't even put the car in park. Jackie finally managed to get out of the car and run back inside her house.

Her mother asked her what happened because Deacon Connelly had come to the picnic looking sweatier than ever and alone. Jackie told her mother that she had gotten a headache and stomachache and declined the invitation when Deacon Connelly had come by to pick her up. Not all a lie, considering the man did make her sick to her stomach. She never told her mother the real reason she didn't come to Greater New Bethel anymore after that. On one hand, it was funny but on another more tragic note, it was so pathetic, what her life had become.

The phone on her nightstand rang. Jackie looked over to check the caller ID and saw that it was an "Out of Area" call. She didn't usually answer those because they were usually salespeople, or worse, bill collectors.

Today, she would answer because it might have something to do with Royce's wedding.

"Hello." All she heard was some breathing on the line and then static. "Hello?" It seemed she had been getting a lot of those kinds of calls lately. If she were the suspicious type, she would wonder who was playing on the phone, but since she didn't have time to think about that now, she chose to forget about it.

Jackie finally sat up in bed. She thought back to yesterday. It had been hell down at the gas company. She had tried to get her desk in order, since she would be off on Friday. It seemed like everyone wanted or needed something ASAP, and Jackie was the only one who could and would deliver on time. She had worked for the gas company for the last twenty-five years and was looking forward to the time when she could retire. She sometimes found her job as a data analyst challenging, what with all the new technology. She made sure she was always aware of the latest gadgets and gizmos, and she learned new applications so quickly that she was often called on to help out her co-workers.

Some of her best times had been with co-workers, especially all the lonely days and nights Jimmy had been out of town. They'd helped her fill the dull hours, and in a lot of ways, some of them were closer than her own family.

First thing Thursday morning her boss, David, had asked her to get the latest numbers from the database she maintained and update the maintenance report, but of course, the computer chose that time to act the fool. It took her over two hours and three calls to the IT department to get it to act right again. She didn't complain much though because she had worked her way up to this position and was thankful for it.

Tony Baldwin, from tech support, came by her office to make sure everything was running smoothly. Tony was some kind of fine too. Dimpled cheeks, smooth chocolate skin, tight body, single, and no kids,. That man knew how to fill out a pair of dark jeans, but he was ten years her junior. No one could understand why she kept turning down his invitations to go out and have a cocktail or two. What she couldn't do with fine-ass Tony, but that was just dreaming, wasn't it?

"Hi, Jackie. How's everything going? Just wanted to make sure you weren't stressing about your work. I know you're getting ready for Royce's wedding. I wouldn't want these old machines around here to get you unfocused."

"Nah, Tony. Everything's going great now. Just knowing you got my back relieves all the stress. Besides, I know who to call when old Bessie here starts acting up," she said with a genuine smile as she patted the computer.

"Great, that's just great! Well, I guess I'll see you at the wedding on Saturday, unless you want to catch dinner and a movie with me after work? That new Will Smith movie is out, and I've heard great reviews," said Tony with smiling dimples lighting up his face.

"Sorry, but still got too much to do this evening, but give me a rain check until after the wedding. Okay? And make sure you sit down front and center, so those bridesmaids of Jessica's can have some eye candy to look at."

"Jackie, you just wait. One day, I'm going get you for all that teasing about my dimples. Come here and let me give you a big old hug for good luck, and I'll see you on Saturday."

As Jackie hugged Tony back, she thought to herself how good it felt to be held in a strong man's arms. It had been way too long. She almost told him she would meet him after work for drinks and whatever, but she chickened out at the last minute. Jackie watched Tony walk away and wondered again how someone that nice could still be single. No kids, good job, so why didn't she jump on it? Too many years' difference in age was the answer she usually gave herself. But really she knew nothing long-term ever came from on-the-job romances.

It was way past time to move on with her life and stop living in the past, but as usual, her mind and her heart differed on everything. And her heart was not the best decision maker. She was still suffering from the decisions she had let it make in the past.

As Jackie was getting dressed for her nail appointment she couldn't believe Friday had actually arrived and she was still holding on to her sanity. Between work yesterday and that crazy scene with Chrystal on Wednesday night, she didn't know whether to laugh hysterically or cry like one of her little grandbabies who didn't get a cookie when they wanted one. *Now, all I have to do is get through the rehearsal this afternoon and the dinner later on. I wonder if Chrystal will show up. She's so unpredictable and unreliable, but Jewel will look so cute as the flower girl if she just does what she's supposed to do.* Jackie thought further about the arrangements for her son's Royce's wedding.

Things would be so different now with Royce getting married. This was the first time in twenty-five years that she would be living alone. In some ways, Jackie was looking forward to it. Thoughts of what to do with Royce's room played through her mind. *I can have my own reading room or even a computer room. Get myself a new setup and redecorate the whole place. Maybe even fix up Chrystal's old room for the grandbabies. Just got to keep Chrystal from nesting here again.* So many possibilities, it was time for a new beginning.

Jackie puttered around in her kitchen making breakfast. She took a steaming cup of Italian sweet cream flavored coffee in her favorite mug and a cherry cheese Danish onto the back patio. She guessed she was just like her mother with the coffee and creamer, but unlike her mother, she needed hers to wake her up in the morning, not put her to sleep at night. Liquor always did a better job of that. The kitchen door opened directly onto the patio, and with just one small step down she was in heaven. She had done so much with the patio over the years, but the one most important reason she bought the house was the rose garden that still bloomed delicious-smelling flowers all around the patio's perimeter.

She and her father had looked at more than a dozen homes in her search for the perfect place. She wanted nothing that reminded her of Jimmy's house in Midtown. It was an old, two-story, Victorian home. It had a lot of charm, but it just wasn't to her liking in the least. Instead, she looked at newer ranch homes in the suburbs.

When Jackie stepped from the kitchen onto the patio for the first time, the realtor smiled, knowing she had made the sale. Jackie had always loved flowers. When Jackie was a child, her mother had often talked to her while she pruned the roses. Ms. Sylvi would tell her all the names and origins of the different roses. When Jackie had looked at the flowers in her own yard, she could hear her mother say, "Now this is an old-fashioned rose. See the double petals. And this here is a tea rose." Jackie loved their smells, especially the lemon-yellow ones.

Jackie had added a trellis to cover the top of the patio, but it still allowed the area to be bathed in mellow sunlight. Blossoming flowers and vines ran up the trellis, and some of the vines had actually run across the top, giving the entire area a nice cool shade. The humming birds were magical, buzzing around the flowers and getting their sweet nectar. She loved to watch them.

This was the calming part of her home. She often came out back to think and commune with nature. The backyard was entirely enclosed with a wooden fence she had added. Privacy was never an issue; she had wonderful neighbors who respected their property. It didn't seem like she had been here for more than ten years, but she had.

A little squirrel ran down the tree in the corner and ran behind a bush nearby, chattering at her the whole while. Jackie didn't mind them too much unless they started digging in her flower beds. Then they were dead meat.

She settled back into her comfy patio furniture and set her mug and pastry on the small table beside her. She had also brought her phone out with her, just in case anyone called. *Yes, this is it. So calm, so peaceful.* She even let the kids play in the yard now and then, as long as they didn't pull up her flowers. Jewel liked to help her deadhead her flowers, but she would get too enthusiastic sometimes and pull the still-blooming petals off. Proudly, she would hand them to Jackie and say, "Look Grandma Jack. I got you pretty flowers." There wasn't much Jackie could say to that but, "Thank you, baby, but next time, let's just look at them and not pull them off the plant."

Jackie's phone rang and she looked at the caller ID. It was her sister, Nancy. "Hi Nancy. What's up? What you got going?" she said, without waiting for her sister to say anything.

"Jackie, please give me time to say something," Nancy said, laughing. "You always do that. How's it going, girl? I know you're ready for tomorrow to be over with. I'm glad I'm just a guest and not the mother of the groom or bride. Hey, I meant to ask you if Jimmy or any of his people are coming to the wedding?"

"Now, you know I haven't had any contact with Jimmy since before Jewel was born, and as far as his side of the family, I've never had much to do with them. Those people never liked me back then, and I don't think anything has changed. Even if it's their grandson and nephew that's getting married, they probably wouldn't lift a finger to come.

"I didn't send them an invitation, but Royce acted a little hesitant when I asked him about the guest list. Since Jessica and her mother were handling everything, I didn't sweat it too much. As long as my side of the family was invited, and y'all sent gifts, I let it be," said Jackie as she laughed out loud.

"But you know it makes me a little sad to think about Royce moving out. That's my baby boy. He's not old enough to take on a wife and family life. He doesn't even wash his own clothes. I do everything for him. He hasn't ever lived by himself, and now he's going to jump into marriage." Jackie stretched her legs as she looked around her beautiful garden.

"And you know a baby will probably be coming nine months later. I can just see it now. 'Ma, the baby won't stop crying and Jessica is crying too. What should I do?'" Jackie shook her head at the image she was painting as she took another sip of her coffee.

"Jackie, stop that. You know that's just selfish. He knows what's best for him, and Jessica seems to be it. Wish them luck, love, and happiness. Stop trying to bust their bubble."

"I'm not trying to discourage him and Jessica, not really, but I do wish they would wait. At least until Jessica graduates from college. I don't want him to take on that entire burden by himself. The girl needs to be bringing in some income too. Even though her parents are practically paying for everything, I just don't feel right about it all."

"Jackie, I think it's really *you* who isn't ready for Royce to move out. Child, let that boy go. He needs a life of his own, not sitting around taking care of his old mama. Jessica can wash his clothes and cook for him too. He doesn't need you to do those things anymore. Besides, they're in love. I can see that with my own eyes every time I look at them. Don't base everything on your marriage to Jimmy. Move on."

Jackie took immediate offense and almost yelled into the phone. "I wish everybody would stop telling me to move on with my life. Chrystal said the same thing to me when she came over here the other night, trying to get me to keep the kids. I am not living in the past. I *have* moved on. What do you all want me to do? Please tell me if you have the master plan."

"Look Jackie, I'm not trying to tell you what to do. I'm sorry if I crossed the line. All I'm saying is that Royce and Jessica are good for each other. Don't worry so much about them."

A little less heated, Jackie said, "I'm just saying that I don't want to see Royce hurt. He's so young and he, he … ah shit. I don't know. I just don't know." Jackie's eyes filled with hot thunderous tears as she looked out over her garden. She suddenly felt so sad. Even her creamed coffee had started to sour in her stomach, and the vibrant colors of her garden became dull and muted.

"Take care of yourself. Get your fat butt out there and get your groove back like Stella," Nancy said. "You always said everybody needs to shake a tail feather now and then. When was the last time you went out on the town? Get some thick long sausage back in your life."

Jackie laughed so hard it brought lilac tears of joy to her eyes, "Get some thick sausage back in my life! Girl, you are too crazy. I do not need any man-meat in my life. I've had enough of that."

Nancy laughed too. "I'm just saying. How about that guy you work with? You know, Tony. From your description, he sounds like just the right spiciness. You know I don't go in for the young ones, but I might just try if you don't jump on it. It would be like robbing the cradle, but what the hell, why not? I'm not telling you to get involved in a long-term relationship. Just get involved in a little nookie-nookie."

"Okay, Nancy. You're making me choke on my coffee with your nonsense, but I understand. I promise you I'll get my groove back like Stella and get some nookie. Okay? As you said, let me get my fat butt up and get ready to get out of here. I'll talk to you later."

"Okay, I'll see you tomorrow morning to help you with your hair. Love you, sis. Bye."

Jackie didn't get up right away. She smiled to herself about what Nancy had said. Maybe she had been holding on to Royce too much. And Tony just might be what she needed. But it was so hard to let go; she knew this most of all. Because even though she didn't want him to, Jimmy came into her mind again.

Friday morning – Royce and Jessica's condo

Royce was tense. He looked at his fiancée Jessica and hunched his shoulders.

He knew what she was going to say before she got the question out. "Royce, what do you think is going on with your sister?"

It was easy to see the tension in his neck and the rigid line of his jaw, as if he were trying to control the words that came from his mouth. "I really don't know, babe, but I do know that somebody has to stop her. She makes Mom so mad with all her foolishness and mess. If the guy Mom said she was hanging with is who I think he is, then big sis is in way over her head."

"What do you mean 'in way over her head'? I thought she was just messing around with her next baby-daddy-to-be. I mean, we all know Chrystal isn't the best when it comes to picking men, but I know she wouldn't do anything to endanger the children. Would she?"

"I hope not Jessica but this guy Smoke isn't just a record producer like Chrystal told Mom. He's one of the biggest meth and crack dealers around. I mean, if what I heard is right, this guy has a whole network of folks spreading this stuff around. Gang activity, prostitution, the whole thing. I pray I'm wrong, but I think it's the same guy."

"Oh baby, I hope you are wrong," Jessica said as she came and sat beside Royce.

"You know Chrystal had some trouble with the stuff a couple years ago, but we all thought she had learned her lesson. Mom had to really go out on a limb to get her out of trouble. I don't think Chrystal will come out ahead if this is the same guy, and I know mom won't."

"Oh, babe, I pray it's not the same guy too, but you're probably right, and it probably is him. Poor Chrystal. I wonder if she knows what she's gotten involved in. I know your sister doesn't really like me. I can tell by how she always calls me Miss Thang, but I don't want anything bad to happen to her. Or your mom. Royce you have to tell her what you think is going on. Please don't let all this mess drop on her head without any warning."

"I'll do what I can. You know Chrystal doesn't listen to nobody but Chrystal, but I'll call her right now."

Feeling worried, Royce picked up his cell phone and called Chrystal. "Hey, Sis. What's going on?"

"Oh, hey Royce. What's up." Royce could hear the hesitation in Chrystal's voice.

"Mom said you were by the other night. Everything okay?" Royce pulled Jessica closer to him and kissed her cheek.

"Yeah. Why you want to know? It wasn't much. I was just asking her about keeping the kids for a little while. But it don't matter now. My plans have changed."

"What? Yeah, I know. Mom said the gig was off in Miami, but we were just wondering about this guy, Smoke. Is everything cool with him? How did you meet him anyway?"

"Man you are too full of questions. For your information he's a friend of Nikki's. Why you all up in my business anyway? You're the one getting married tomorrow. You need to take care of your own business and stop worrying about mine. I got my stuff together."

Royce shifted the phone to his other ear and said, "I thought you stopped hanging with Nikki? But, I was just asking, that's all."

"Well, you need to take care of Miss Thang and stay out of my way. Okay."

"Yeah, I just don't want anything to happen to you and the kids. I know you can handle your own business, but I—Okay. Well, we'll see you later."

Royce shrugged. "Well, that went nowhere. She about told me to mind my own business and that I needed to just take care of Miss Thang." Royce shrugged his shoulders again and rubbed his chin as he thought over his next move.

"Oh, Royce, you tried. She's so stubborn and secretive about her life. I know it's just a front, but I wish she would open up to you. You are her only brother after all. And what was that about a Nikki?"

"Nikki is the daughter of Mom's cousin Sheila. So I guess we're second cousins. Chrystal and she were always running around together, getting into all kinds of trouble. That's who she was hanging with when she got into drugs. Anyway, she said Nikki hooked her up with this

Smoke guy." Royce ran his hand over his eyes and sighed. "Jessica, I want to help but I just don't know what to do. Chrystal is a big girl. I'll see what I can do though. Maybe I can talk to this guy Smoke."

Jessica absent-mindedly rubbed Royce's arm. Royce suddenly swung Jessica up in a big hug. "Okay, let's talk about something else. Too much of this Chrystal conversation is a real downer."

"Well, okay. What about your little surprise guest? Is everything still going to happen? I know your mom will be so surprised. But I don't want too many things to surprise her though."

"Yes, the surprise is still on. It took some tracking to locate them, but it will be totally worth it to see the look on Mom's face. She always talked about how they were best friends back in the day and how much help to her when she needed it most, especially at work. So I think it will be just what she needs. I kind of remember them being around when I was little. I know a couple of times they would come over and Mom would be so happy. Okay, let's get some lunch and spend the last day of our unmarried lives having fun. What do you say, Mrs. Soon-to-be Jessica Mattock? Want to kiss a soon-to-be-married man?"

"You bet. Lay one on me, baby. I always wanted to know what it feels like to mess around with an almost married man. But I don't want you to be upset and I don't want our marriage to start out under a black cloud. I just feel like something is just not right."

Royce also felt the beginnings of a steady burn in his chest that had nothing to do with the upcoming nuptials but everything to do with his mother and sister. He could see a sheen of tears in Jessica's eyes and he had a terrible feeling that something really, really bad was about to happen. And knowing Chrystal the black cloud that Jessica feared might just turn into a hurricane.

5

What's the color of your tears?
Ashy and pale, denude of laughter and joy
Opening death's door to all your fears
Pulling on tight strings as if you're a toy

Jackie left the nail salon with her fingers and toes newly manicured. Nothing flashy, just a French mani/pedi but it did make her feel so elegant. She usually went in for the blues, yellows, and greens, but this time she wanted to make sure she looked as sophisticated as Jessica's mother, Natalie Reese. Anytime she had to meet with the Reese's, Jackie felt underdressed and so urban.

Not that the Reese's came from backgrounds so different from hers. It was the way they presented themselves that made her self-conscious. Natalie always had her hair groomed in the latest style. Lately, she sported a long bob that gently brushed her shoulders. The reddish-blonde color highlighted her creole complexion. Of course, it would be Natalie's natural hair color, and the woman had the nerve to look thirty-something when Jackie knew she had to be pushing fifty, just like Jackie was.

While Jackie loved her natural curly hair, with just enough texture to make it sit high on her head, she knew it made her look a little bohemian. Not that she minded, but some people were so prejudiced about hair type. And she knew she didn't look old for forty-nine, but she knew she looked forty-something, and that was the rub. Small and slender, Natalie made Jackie feel like a buffalo every time she had to stand beside her. Not that Jackie was that tall, but at five-six to Natalie's five feet, she looked and felt like a giant.

Natalie and Jessica could have passed for sisters instead of mother and daughter. Jessica had the same creole coloring as her mother, but where Natalie wore her hair in a bob, Jessica had long, curly, dark brown hair.

And Earl Reese, at six-two, had that dark skin that looked like smooth, ageless chocolate, and he towered over his tiny wife like her knight in shining armor. They appeared to be the perfect couple and so in love. They both were realtors and owned rental property all over Atlanta and Decatur. They were even giving Royce and Jessica one of their condos to live in, not to mention paying for most of the wedding and a honeymoon in Bermuda. What more could you ask from your in-laws?

Jackie made her way back to her canyon brown Porsche Cayenne. She wasn't usually in to flashy cars, but for once, she had given in to this one guilty pleasure. Okay, two guilty pleasures because designer shoes were also on the list. She had always liked foreign cars, a throwback to Jimmy, she guessed. He always drove the latest and coolest car. He definitely had good taste when it came to material goods.

She wondered if Jimmy knew Royce was getting married. She hadn't talked to him in almost five years and wasn't even sure where he stayed now. She had long since stopped driving by the house in Midtown, especially since the "For Sale" and subsequent "Sold" signs went up. She hadn't received any money from him since Royce graduated college, and that was over a year ago. She hadn't wanted alimony in the divorce settlement. Nancy told her she was crazy for not going after it.

"Jackie, take that damn man to the cleaners," Nancy had told her. "Get all you can get and then some. He owes you. You stayed in that marriage way too long. Men! I told you not to trust them. Now see, he just leaves you high and dry." Nancy didn't even know the whys or how's of the divorce, but she stood firmly in Jackie's corner.

As usual, Ms. Sylvi was on Jimmy's side, "Now, Jackie, just be calm. He's the children's daddy. Don't worry. I know he'll do right by them."

But her daddy also stood behind Jackie one hundred percent. "Baby, don't worry about nothing. You know me and your mama will be right here for you for whatever you need. You just put your trust in the Lord, and everything will be all right," said Buddy as he hugged her tightly to his chest.

Jackie had only wanted Jimmy to pay child support until both children graduated college. She had primary custody, and Jimmy was given visitation every other weekend and some holidays, which he might have taken advantage of ten times in all those years.

She'd also wanted her equal share of the bank accounts and assets, which turned out to be a tidy sum. She'd had no idea he was worth that much or had so many different accounts. And the final thing she'd asked for was the BMW she was driving at the time.

Jackie avoided mentioning Jimmy's name when Jessica's family asked about Royce's dad. She remembered Royce saying not to worry about his dad because everything was taken care of. She never got around to asking him exactly what he meant by that.

Okay, now on to check on the cake and flowers. In a lot of ways, she was glad she was the mother of the groom. She didn't have to do nearly as much as the bride's mother. She had taken on the chores of finding the place to hold the rehearsal dinner, making sure the cake was delivered on time, and ensuring each member of the wedding party had the correct flowers. Really, there wasn't much to do since Royce and Jessica were having the wedding at a wonderful hall that fixed up everything Jessica and her mother had picked out to Natalie's exacting specifications. It wasn't a huge wedding, what with just three bridesmaids and groomsmen, but it was very sophisticated, even elaborate if you asked Jackie.

As she eased into her Porsche, her cell phone started to play a tune. She had downloaded a sexy little ringtone that was popular now. She could never remember who the artist was, but she had to admit it was catchy and gave a real boost to her spirits.

"Now, where has that damn phone gotten itself to? Hello? Hello?" There was no response.

"How the hell do I get rid of 'out of area' calls on my cell phone? I'm so tired of people playing on my phone. People don't have anything better to do these days?" Jackie looked around to see if anyone saw her talking to herself and breathed a sigh of relief that the sidewalk looked empty. She started up her car and eased out of the parking spot into traffic and headed for the bakery.

"The cakes look fantastic." The wedding cake was to die for. It had three square layers, each turned at a different angle. The design gave the whole thing a look like a multi-tiered, frosted mountain. The groom's cake wasn't too shabby either. It was Royce's favorite of course—chocolate—but with a streaming cup of coffee outlined in frosting on the top. Royce and Jessica had met over a cup of coffee at Atlanta University Center, and it held a special significance for them. She couldn't help but smile at the baker's assistant as she lowered the top on the groom's cake. "Deliver them to the Faithful Dove, in Stone Mountain, by one o'clock tomorrow afternoon. Remember it's for the Reese-Mattock wedding at three. Thanks again." Jackie felt on top of the world for a change. *It looks like things are finally going to work out well*, she thought. *Yeah, things are finally going the way it should. Thank you Lord.* But of course she was wrong again.

It was Friday afternoon and Jackie needed a nap before it was time to go the hall and rehearse the wedding. She didn't have to be there until five. *I'll just stretch out across this bed and catch a little bit of shut-eye.*

Ring, ring, ring, went the phone. Jackie startled awake and looked at the bedside clock. She couldn't believe it was 4:30 already. She jumped for the phone and didn't bother to look at the caller ID. "Hello."

"You know looks can be deceiving. Just when you think you know someone, they flip on you. Everything ain't always how it seems. You need to check out what people around you really doing. Just thought I'd let you know."

"What? What did you say? Who is this?" Jackie looked at the dead phone in her hand. "What the hell was that about? Who the hell keeps calling me with this stupid shit?" This time the caller ID read Unknown Caller. The caller had sort of sounded like a woman or a man with a very high-pitched voice, but she didn't recognize the voice and the caller ID wasn't giving her any hints.

Jackie stumbled her way into her bathroom and washed the sleep out of her eyes. She stood looking at herself in the mirror. Forty-nine years and counting. Her birthday was in November, and the big five-oh was staring her in the face. *Not too bad,* she thought. She still had a pretty good shape, just thicker around the middle. She spun around and looked at her rear in the mirror. *Girl, that butt is still sitting high and you ain't lost it all yet.* Face, not bad. She loved her big, pouty lips. A few lines that weren't there a couple of years ago, but all in all, not bad. Hair may not be like Ms. Natalie's, but she thought her golden brown natural hair wasn't too shabby. It had taken years to get all that perm out of it. Now she had a nice, shoulder-length, curly, twisty do that flattered her high cheekbones and dark brown eyes. Jimmy never did know what a real woman was. *Ah shit, why I am still thinking about him?*

Jackie quickly changed out of her house dress and slipped into a rose-colored pants outfit. She added a dash of her favorite perfume and a burgundy lipstick; silver, dangling earrings and silver bracelets completed her outfit. *I'll just step into these Jimmy Choo's to add a splash of style 'cause them folks ain't got nothing on me, and they better get ready.*

Jackie drove up to the rehearsal with the sounds of Barry White playing on her XM satellite station. She didn't know why she gravitated to the oldies station, but it always seemed to put her in a good mood. This afternoon didn't need much coaxing to get her happy. Royce was getting married to Jessica tomorrow, and all was right with the world. She looked around the parking lot and noticed several familiar cars and even more that she had never seen before. Jessica's little blue Volkswagen bug was parked right beside Royce's older model Ford Explorer.

Jessica's parents didn't play when it came to their daughter. There would be no premarital cohabitation. Jessica and Royce steadfastly maintained separate residences. Royce stayed at Jackie's house and Jessica at her parent's. Jackie didn't mind that too much. Although no one knew what went on when Royce and Jessica were together and alone.

She believed young people moved much too fast these days. Meet online one day, have a drink and another drink. Next thing you knew, they had an apartment together. She thought Jessica's parents were a bit too protective of her. Everyone needed to get out and shake a few tail feathers now and then, as Nancy had reminded her, but being the mother of the groom, she couldn't complain too much.

Jackie wished she had kept tighter reins on Chrystal. Maybe then Chrystal would have never gotten involved with drugs among other things. The whole police arrest and court room drama was still too fresh in her mind. It had been almost two years but her failure when it came to Chrystal still hurt sharper than a knife. ... But there was no point in wishing for what wasn't. It was time to move on.

~

Friday evening before the wedding

"So, Jackie, Royce tells us you have a special surprise for the wedding," said Earl with a small smile on his face. Jackie looked quickly from Royce to Jessica to Natalie. Jewel took that moment to grab a roll from the basket on the dinner table and slowly but methodically break it into tiny, little pieces.

Everyone was smiling and having a great dinner. The young friends of Jessica who were the bridesmaids, chatted it up with the friends of Royce serving as his best man and groomsmen. Royce had swung by and picked up Ms. Sylvi, and she was chatting with Jessica's grandmother, but they both stopped talking to hear what Earl Reese was saying.

What in the world is Earl talking about? Jackie extracted the pieces of bread from Jewel's grasp.

"No, Grandma Jack. I want to eat it," said Jewel. She started to cry and whimper.

Jackie took her time in calming Jewel as she tried to come up with something that made sense. She struggled to remember if Royce had told her something about this surprise.

Royce shook his head at her with a secretive smile on his face. Jackie wanted to smack her only son. Instead she hurriedly tried to come up with some sort of answer that would satisfy Earl. "Royce, you know we agreed to keep a 'wait and see' policy." She pasted a too-sweet smile on her face. What the hell was happening to her? Was she having a stroke or something? She couldn't remember a thing. She hadn't talked to Royce about any special surprises. She just hoped he would go along with what she was saying.

"Mom, you know the special surprise we talked about." Royce leaned back in his chair, absentmindedly playing with Jessica's hair.

"Well, Earl, it wouldn't be a surprise if I told you now, would it?" Jackie said. "You'll just have to wait and see like everyone else." There, now take that, Mr. Reese.

"Touché, Jackie. I told him the same thing," said a laughing Natalie as she playfully smacked Earl on his arm.

"Okay. Everyone wants to gang up on me. I just asked a question, that's all. Royce help me out. I was only repeating what you said." Earl popped a piece of bread into his mouth.

"Who me? I know when to surrender," said Royce. "We all will just have to wait and see. Right, Mom?"

What kind of game was going on here? Jessica looked at Jackie as if Jackie had the answers to all life's questions. Jackie thought everything had gone so well with the rehearsal. Everyone knew exactly when to come in and where to stand, and the timing was down pat. Now what kind of shit were they trying to start?

Chrystal, dressed in a modest outfit for a change, regular jeans and a nice blouse, had even shown up with Jewel and had gotten the little girl to walk down the aisle just as she was supposed to. She had left Oro and Jade with Chantrelle, who apparently had gotten over her flu. And Chantrelle even let Chrystal use her car.

Jackie knew that whole sick with the flu story had been just that, a made-up tale. But Chrystal had surprised Jackie by not only showing up but bringing a little basket for Jewel. She told the little girl to playact as if she were tossing out flowers. Jewel was perfect for her part.

Of course, before anyone could comment on anything, Chrystal had gotten a mysterious text, grabbed Jewel, shoved her into Jackie's arm, and left in a fit; mumbling, "They so trifling. They think they gonna play me." Jackie was so flustered by Chrystal's behavior that, for once, she couldn't say a thing.

Friday night – the Bluff

"I told y'all, I ain't got it. Smoke was taking care of everything. He didn't leave me with nothing. Nikki told me all I had to do was come down here and give y'all this package. I didn't even look in it. I don't know how much was supposed to be there."

Chrystal couldn't believe this shit was actually happening to her. She didn't have no ten thousand dollars, and she sure as hell didn't have the stuff. In fact, she wasn't even sure what was going on. She thought, *this has got to be some Nikki mess, trying to set me up.* All she could think of now was what her mother always told her: "It's much easier not to do than to undo."

Duck, the so called leader of the group thumped Chrystal hard on her head with his fist and said, "Well, y'all, I guess we're just going to have to see what we can do with this rabbit. This couple of dollars don't even come close to what we agreed to with Smoke. You know, baby girl, ain't no free rides. You always got to pay somehow, some way."

For the first time in her life, Chrystal understood real fear. She looked at the people who Nikki had sent her to in the Bluff and wanted to strangle that bitch. These weren't just the pretend thugs she was used to dealing with. This guy Duck was involved in for real gangster shit, and she couldn't talk her way out of it. Duck looked like the worst evil villain she had ever seen. He had on a too tight tee-shirt with a black laughing skull emblazoned across the front. Another one of the gang members looked like his pants were sagging so low he was gonna trip every time he took a step. And the used-up trick they had with them was old enough to be her mother and didn't have five good teeth in her mouth. Nothing but crackheads.

And where was that fat fool when you needed him? He was always talking big shit to her, and now what? He had told her to be cool. He had her, he said. What a fool she was. She should have known better to let Nikki talk her into this shit. Easy money my ass. If Nikki and Smoke were in this together, she was really screwed this time.

"Wait a minute, y'all. I think I can get in touch with Smoke. Just give me a second to find out what's going on. My girl Nikki told me y'all was cool with everything." Chrystal frantically hit Nikki back on her cell. Her fingers shook so badly she could hardly hold the phone. *That bitch better answer*, she thought, and to her overwhelming relief, Nikki finally did.

"Girl, where Smoke? These people keep asking about where the stuff is. They say there's not enough money here."

Nikki popped her gum and answered, "Chrystal, what you calling me for?"

Frantically Chrystal yelled into the phone, "Is Smoke there with you? I need to talk to him real quick."

Nikki answered, "yeah and what about it. You supposed to be handling our business not calling me. But hold on, here Smoke."

"Yeah, whatever. Hey, Smoke. What's up with this? These guys say the count ain't right. I told them I didn't know anything about that. You need to talk to them, because they don't believe nothing I tell them. You need to tell them yourself."

Chrystal was so afraid that she didn't wait for Smoke to answer. She handed the phone to the one they called Duck. "Yo, man, we got your rabbit down here, but I wants my money. This ain't even the right count. You know what I mean. Yeah, well, you better get your black ass down here, or honey gonna be swimming in the Chattahoochee."

Duck looked at Chrystal and laughed. "You know you one pretty bitch, but we want our money, so I would hate to see you not looking as pretty as you were when you came in here. Fat ass Smoke better get up off his monkey ass and get here quick. I'll give him twenty minutes before I start hitting."

Duck cracked his knuckles, saggy jeans belched loudly and the crackhead ho looked at Chrystal like she was her next meal. As a silent crystal tear rolled out the corner of her eye, Chrystal thought, *that's the same thing I hope and pray too. Oh Lord, what a shitty-ass way to make a living.*

Friday night

All Jackie could think about as she got into her Porsche was what in the world was going on with Royce. He must have grinned at her the entire evening. She had said enough good-nights to last a life time. Everyone had cleared out the restaurant parking lot but her.

They'd all acted strangely during the rehearsal dinner to Jackie. Even Ms. Perfect Natalie had reached up to give Jackie a hug as if to encourage her. With her perfect hair and perfect slip dress, which Jackie couldn't even get one butt cheek into, and her size-five, tiny feet encased in Manolo Blahniks, the woman probably didn't weight a hundred pounds soaking wet. Still, there she was, hugging Jackie as if to console her, but about what? Why was she the one to pity now? What the hell was going on around her?

She thought back to the phone call earlier that day. "You know looks can be deceiving. Everything ain't always how it seems." Or something like "People ain't always what they seem." What people? Who was doing something they shouldn't be, and why did someone think she needed to know? And the question-and-answer quiz from Earl. What in the world was going on?

She needed some soothing music to get her head back in a good place. The Isleys were playing on her XM with one of her favorites, "Voyage to Atlantis." She leaned her head on the headrest and exhaled deeply. Just trying to stay a step ahead of the Reese's, Royce, and of course Chrystal had aged her. Jackie felt all of her forty-nine years and then some. It didn't seem like it should have taken such a toll on her, but she guessed she was tired from all that had gone on this past week.

If I do say so myself, I think I handled that very well. It was only ten o'clock, but Jackie felt like it was midnight. Royce had finally gotten a text from Chrystal, saying she wouldn't be back. Ms. Sylvi had volunteered to keep Jewel overnight, and Royce was taking them both home. Jackie had Jewel's outfit at her house, so she would just go over to her mother's, where everyone was to meet anyway, a little earlier tomorrow. Nancy had rented a van to take everybody to the wedding. She was supposed to come over to Jackie's house first and help Jackie with her hair.

It was funny how Chrystal's grandma had a better relationship with Chrystal's children than she had with Chrystal herself. She had clothes, toys, and food, for them at her house, and she even had a bedroom fully furnished with a crib and toddler beds.

Ever since Jackie's father had been killed in a three-car pile-up, neither she nor her mother had been the same. Ms. Sylvi needed her great-grandchildren to bring life back into her home. Jackie often felt that three little ones was just too much for one seventy-four-year-old woman, and it made her feel even guiltier about her lack of support.

Ms. Sylvi lost her joy two years ago. Jackie had been over her parents' house for dinner when Ms. Sylvi declared she needed some hazelnut creamer to go with her after-dinner coffee. She always swore that it settled her stomach and put her right to sleep every time. Unfortunately, that Friday night, they were all out of creamer. Buddy, a doting husband even after fifty-two years of marriage, couldn't say no to his bride.

"You sit back with your mother, and I'll run down to the store and get some," Buddy replied to Jackie when she volunteered to go get it. "Your mother loves for you to tell her all about them crazy folks down at your job. I'll be right back."

Buddy leaned down and gave Ms. Sylvi a gentle kiss on the cheek and whispered something that made her blush and brought a twinkle to her light brown eyes. The two women relaxed at the kitchen table as he grabbed his cap and went out the door. Jackie looked on with love and, yes, envy in her heart at the tender way her dad still treated her mother.

Her mother was still a beautiful woman. She had a full head of silver hair that almost made a halo around her face. For seventy-something years old, she hardly had any wrinkles and her back was as straight as ever.

Jackie's father was tall and strong still. In her eyes, he was just as handsome as he was when she was a little girl and he would swing her high in the air. He hadn't lost any hair either, and his dark brown skin complemented her mother's lighter hue. What a beautiful couple they made.

She thought of how both her parents still maintained such love and respect for each other. *That's all I ever wanted in my marriage, a man who loved me, his family, and God. A man who treated me with respect and tenderness. A man like my daddy.* Neither she nor her mother realized that man they both loved and admired would never see another day.

They sat around the table playing cards, trying not to fear, for over an hour and a half. They both knew something was terribly wrong. The entire round trip shouldn't have taken more than thirty minutes. Neither her father nor her mother carried cell phones. They claimed they were too old for such foolishness, and usually, where one was the other was right beside them. Jackie wished her dad had a cell phone now so she could at least contact him and tell him to not worry about the creamer. Just come on home.

"You know, Jackie, I bet your daddy is down at that store and forgotten what I sent him for." Ms. Sylvi tried to laugh but it came out in shaky breaths. "He does that sometimes. He'll come home scratching his head and apologizing. I just kiss him and tell him it's okay. I didn't want it anyway." She ended on a long sigh.

"Hey, Mom. Why don't we go see what's taking him so long? I bet you're right and he has forgotten what he went for." Jackie felt such an overwhelming urge to cry, but she knew she needed to be strong for her mother because she knew in her heart that the worst had happened.

Much later that night, as they sat in the lobby of the emergency room, hugging each other, Nancy came running in. "Oh my God, Jackie, Mom...What, why, oh my God! I got here as fast as I could. I was just watching TV when you called. I got my neighbor Chris to drive me over. My nerves, oh Lord my nerves are so bad. I didn't trust myself to drive, so Chris drove me. She's parking the car. Oh God, Jackie, what happened?" Nancy had lost every bit of the composure she normally had, and her cheeks were wet with tears. Nancy looked a lot like her father in that she was tall and had the same chocolate skin color. But her facial features were almost identical to her mother's. She had a very short hair style that was wavy and a beautiful silver color. But now her hair was disheveled from where she constantly ran her hands over her hair.

"Come on and sit down, Nancy. The doctor was just out here and said they were finishing up with Daddy and we could go in to see him in a little bit." Jackie never stopped rocking with her arms around her mother as she told Nancy the news.

In a sing-song voice, Jackie continued. "Daddy hadn't come back from the grocery store, so Mom, I, we thought we would go look for him. And we went down the street, and you know that intersection at North and Lucky Street where everybody runs the light. And anyway, we came up to that intersection and police cars and fire trucks and lights and sirens and people and smashed up cars and trucks . . ."

Ms. Sylvi let out an anguished moan and shook all over as Jackie continued her story. "Well, they wouldn't let us get close in the car, and we jumped out and ran down the street, and they still wouldn't let us get close enough, but I could see Daddy's truck, and it was smoking and crushed up, and another car was flipped over the front end, and another car was smashed into the side and ... " Jackie took a huge breath and sobbed.

"No, Jackie, no. Mom. Oh please, God, please. I can't believe this. Please tell me this isn't happening," pleaded Nancy.

"We told them that was our father, Mom's husband. And they said he and the other victims had been taken to Grady and we should go there, and now here we are." Jackie stopped rocking her mother and stared at the door waiting for the doctor to come back.

Nancy jumped up as Chris came running through the door. "Chris, Daddy is, oh Chris, I don't know, but it doesn't look good." Nancy broke down further as Chris hugged her.

"Stinson family, you can come with me now." They all followed the doctor through a set of double doors to a curtained-off part of the emergency room. Machines were everywhere, with tubing and flickering monitors and beeping sounds all around a hospital bed. There lay Buddy, with so many wires and tubes and bandages that he was almost unrecognizable. They could see part of his face had been bleeding and another part looked burned but had light gauze covering it. One eye was completely bandaged over. He didn't look anything like the laughing, joking Buddy everyone knew.

Ms. Sylvi went to the side of the bed where she could get closest to her husband. She took Buddy's free hand and rubbed it against her cheek. Her honey colored tears wet his fingers as she clasped them to her face. Buddy opened the one eye that wasn't bandaged and tried to turn his head towards his wife.

"Buddy, what you gone and done now? You weren't supposed to be gone this long. You know it's way past your bedtime. Come on and get up." She could barely get the words out and ended on a strangled sob.

All Jackie, Nancy, and Chris could do was huddle together and hold on to each other. "Sylvi, what you cry-crying 'bout?" croaked Buddy from the bed. He tried to cup Ms. Sylvi's chin, but his fingers just wouldn't work. "You know it's all right. You gonna be all right. I guess I won't get to bed on time tonight. Don't you forget I have always loved you and always will. Don't you worry, everything gonna be . . . ."

"Buddy, don't you dare leave me. Buddy, do you hear me? Buddy, please! Please, doctor, do something for my, for Buddy!" Low sobbing was all that could be heard from Jackie and Nancy.

The doctor came around to the other side of the bed to check one of the machines hooked up to Buddy's chest. Then, he went to the curtain and asked one of the nurses to come inside. "Ladies," he said to Buddy's family, "please wait outside for a moment. I'm afraid there isn't anything else we can do for Mr. Stinson."

He said, death is not the final door
She bent her head to his last breath
One silent tear traced a finishing descent
As two smiles stayed frozen in place

Her mind flew down twisting corridors
Innocent and undamaged from loving
Too young to know better, too old to care
Promises made and somehow he kept

6

What's the color of your tears?
Brackish white that fades into light
Somber browns full of anger and fears
Faded fuchsia blending into the night

Late Friday night – Jackie's house

Jackie let herself into her solemnly quiet house. It seemed as if something was absent already, and the wedding hadn't even taken place yet. Her home was missing Royce, and after tomorrow it would never be the same again. She exhaled a deep breath that she hadn't been aware she was holding. She hadn't even made it through the kitchen when the tears clouded up, ready to release a purple downpour.

She set the alarm to 'at home.' Even if Royce came home, he could reset it. But she really didn't expect him because his best man and groomsmen were taking him out for his last night of bachelorhood. She stopped by Royce's room and stuck her head in. There wasn't much of him left. He and Jessica had moved most of their stuff to the condo. His wedding clothes, a beautiful dove gray morning coat, hung on the closet door. She went over and fingered the material. So many years, and what did she have to show for them?

She was tired, so bone-weary tired that she barely made it to her bedroom before she slipped out of her shoes and tossed them in a corner. "Sorry, Mr. Choo. Didn't mean any disrespect," Jackie mumbled. She saw the message light flashing on her phone. *Who's been calling now?* She punched the play button.

"You should wonder how Chrystal gets her money," an anonymous voice said. "Maybe she earns it some other way, like on her back or her knees. Whatever the trick wants. Just thought you should know."

What in the world is going on? She didn't feel like hearing this shit. She still couldn't catch the voice, but somebody was trying to tell on Chrystal. What was Chrystal doing now, and who was so stupid that they thought Jackie didn't already know?

Next, she went through her bathroom and into her closet and shucked off her clothes. She didn't feel like a shower tonight, maybe a long, hot bath. As she waited for the tub to fill and added her favorite bath salts, she sucked in a deep breath and slowly exhaled. Jackie frowned as she thought about the place in which she now found herself.

Was she really living, or had the past few years only been a dismal facsimile of life? She was just barely hanging on, a passive observer. She knew her present state of mind was probably not the best for contemplating the meaning of her existence, but something was nagging at her so she had no choice but to examine it. It was like that little piece of skin that turned hard and sharp right at the corner of your fingernail, a hangnail, an irritant.

Have I wasted the last twenty-five years of my life? Here she was, almost fifty, and no happier than when she was twenty-four. What had she been doing for the last twenty-five years? Was her purpose to only be a hangnail, an irritant, unnecessary and useless, a thing nobody wanted or needed?

Jackie stepped into her large tub and sank down into the hot water. At first, it was "If I could just find a good man," then it became "If I could just have a baby," and then finally, "Lord, just get me out of this mess!" Then everything would be fine, no worries. But it hadn't turned out that way, not at all.

She, Jackie Stinson Mattock, was a liar and a Jezebel. She had lied to everyone who meant anything in her life. She had even lied to herself. Telling herself that what she was doing was to save her marriage. She had the nerve to wonder what was wrong with Chrystal and why was she so promiscuous. At least Chrystal had an excuse; she had a lying slut for a mother, and a gay, cheating-ass father. The apple doesn't fall far from the tree.

Jackie sank deeper into the tub until her breasts were almost submerged. She took her washcloth and scrubbed at her face. *Maybe if I rub hard enough, I won't cry*, she thought. But it didn't do any good. The tears fell anyway. Big ugly, sloppy tears, full of sadness and remorse. Loud groans and moans of anguish rushed out of her mouth as the tears rushed in to fuel them. She dragged her hands over her nose and mouth, her eyes, anywhere to make the memories stop. But they came flooding back, just like her colored tears.

Despair, like a sleek black cat, sits in my heart
I fear life, I see only the blackness of its parts
Pain and failure are all I have to share
To my horror, I have lost my very self
I only sit and stare

Twenty-four years ago

She hadn't meant for any of it to happen, but Eric had been there when times were so hard for her. She would come to work, exhausted from her sleepless nights. She had only been married a little over a year, but she knew something was wrong. Her husband not only didn't spend much time at home, but he hardly ever touched her. They were still in the honeymoon stage, and she figured they may have made love ten times that year. And then, that couldn't really be called love-making. For her it was desperation and despair that drove her, and no matter how hard she tried, Jimmy wasn't that into it. From foreplay to climax, the whole disappointing encounter may have taken five minutes. She knew that wasn't normal. Jimmy would jump up out of bed and rush into the bathroom when they were finished, almost as if he had to wash off her scent. All she heard was the water running, and all she could do was cry.

Jackie would go to work and sit in her office, staring blindly at her paperwork, trying to come up with some way to save her marriage. Eric Henderson had the office right next to hers. He supervised a group of customer service reps for the gas company. She really liked Eric. In fact, everyone liked Eric. He was just one of those guys who got along with everybody.

Eric had worked his way up in the gas company. He started out as a meter reader. He didn't have the fancy degrees and prestigious college background like Jimmy, but he was such a nice guy. And no, he didn't drive expensive foreign cars or live in the best trendy neighborhood. He drove a Toyota and lived in Riverdale. But there was something so real about Eric that he was hard to overlook.

All the customer service reps held their breath and gave him adoring eyes when he came by. They said he was so nice and so tall and good looking, a real pleasure to work with, which Jackie knew was absolutely true. They all wanted him for their supervisor if they could only choose.

Eric came in at least once a week and invited her to lunch, and she accepted. He insisted on paying no matter where they went. Always the perfect gentleman, he opened doors for her and seated her at the table. They talked about everything and nothing. It was easy, no pressure, and he told her the most ridiculous jokes. They kept her laughing all through lunch. It kept her mind off Jimmy and what she didn't have.

Eric had the most striking eyes. They were a brilliant hazel color, almost golden, and he had the most beautiful smile. It lit up his face when he was happy, which seemed to be always. Along with the hazel eyes came the reddish-brown hair. He often joked, when she asked him about his ancestry, that his great-grandfather was Irish and his great-grandmother was Cherokee. He never actually said what his racial background was. No matter what, he was one good-looking black man, and he was very, very married.

One day, Jackie was so distraught that the tears started up while she was trying to update some new employee information in her files. She became so frustrated that she threw the papers at the wall. Eric stuck his head in the door and asked if she needed any help. Jackie couldn't hold it in any longer, and the tears overflowed and gushed from her eyes like a hurricane.

"Jackie, what's wrong? I know my favorite person in this office isn't in here letting this paper get the best of her." Eric tried to make light of it, but Jackie didn't stop crying, so he came in and closed the door. "Jackie, please, what can I do to help you? You're breaking my heart."

"I don't know if anybody can help me. My husband, my life—Eric you really don't want to know. Everything is so messed up." Eric hugged her, trying to give some comfort.

"Jackie, here's some tissue. Why don't you just start from the beginning? I have time. I have all day if you need it."

It took over an hour for the whole story to unfold. Jackie whimpered and cried off and on as she described the marriage she now found herself in. "Oh, Eric, I want a baby so badly. I just know that will bring Jimmy back home. But our love life ... I don't know how to even describe it. It's pitiful, that's what it is. I'll never have a baby at this rate."

"Jackie, you're an intelligent, beautiful woman. Don't let Jimmy's disinterest make you think differently. I know if I had a woman like you, I would never leave the bedroom." Eric laughed and touched her on her hand. He gently touched her cheek, where the tears were drying. and gave her a small kiss there.

"You don't have to say those things to make me feel better. I know I'm hardly all that. Besides, I've met your wife, and she's gorgeous.

A real ten, so just stop." Jackie was finally starting to feel better, and the tears had slowed to a fine mist, sticking to her eyelashes like dew drops. She couldn't believe Eric had kissed her, and she touched her cheek where the kiss still lingered. Even more, she wanted him to do it again.

Eric shook his head. "No, seriously, looks can be deceiving. Remember I met Jimmy also, but see how it is for you. I thought you guys had the perfect marriage, but it seems I was wrong. It's not much different for me. Lisa is beautiful, and she loves beautiful things, clothes, cars, and people, whatever. There's nothing wrong with that, but she's one of those people who's just not satisfied with one when two or three or five would be better, and that includes men. I have about as much passion in my home as you do.

"Lisa is . . . just Lisa. When we married, I knew she was self-centered and childish, but I thought, as the years went by, she would mature. Now after five years, I guess I was wrong. And kids, Lisa says kids are not for the beautiful people. They make you age too fast. I have love for Lisa, but there's something missing in our marriage that neither Lisa nor I can find."

"Oh, Eric, I'm so sorry. I never would have guessed. You always seem so happy, and Lisa is so gorgeous that I just knew you guys had everything I wanted. I was always jealous of Lisa. So many times I wanted to trade places with her. Never mind. I shouldn't have said that." It made Jackie so sad to think Eric's marriage wasn't any better than hers that she started tearing up again.

"No, don't apologize. Believe it or not, I felt the same way. Sitting here in this office right beside yours, I often fantasized about you and me. I knew it was wrong, but there isn't anything I wouldn't do for you. So now, Ms. Jackie, please tell me what I can do to put a smile on your beautiful face." Eric took her face in his large hands and gently kissed her trembling lips. "Go ahead. You only have to ask."

I would lie down at night for you
I would fill the ragged holes in your soul for you
Taste your very essence and cling to you
Love you 'til my last breath for you

~⌒

Late Friday night – Chrystal's house

It was late, and Chrystal wanted to go to bed. She had just gotten back home. Calvin or Smoke had followed her in his escalade from the Bluff. She was so upset she could barely drive, and she jumped at every police car she saw. She just knew they could tell she had been up to no good and had violated her probation. She'd at least had the presence of mind to text Royce and tell him she wouldn't be coming back tonight. *This is crazy,* she thought. *I can't keep on this way. I don't want to end up like that crazy looking crackhead. Please, Lord, if you give me another chance, I promise I'll do what I should have done years ago.*

She was still nursing her cheek where Duck had hit her. Smoke had barely made it in time. Those fools were about to mess her up bad. They were the kind of people who enjoyed their work too much. She could tell they were upset they didn't have time to hurt her more.

Chrystal finally understood that she couldn't keep getting involved with these criminals. And now this fool Calvin expected her to have sex with him. She went over to her hiding place behind the refrigerator, picked up her Glock, and tucked it into the back of her jeans. She was glad, for once, that he wasn't paying her any attention.

Smoke sat down at the kitchen table, making himself at home. He checked his cell phone for messages, never looking up. "I told you to just do what I tell you and nothing else, but your stupid ass had to go and talk some shit to grown folks." Smoke finally looked up at Chrystal as if she was some kind of fool. "I see you just want to do your own shit. Bitch, you better learn to respect grown folks."

"I know you didn't just call me a bitch. I ain't your bitch, and you better remember that, with your monkey ass. You got the nerve to talk to me like that after everything I've been through tonight? I did everything Nikki told me to. You need to talk to her. How was I to know those thugs were going to play some shit like that? They didn't have to hit me to prove they were men. I'm not your plaything. I'm a grown-ass woman, and—"

"Then you better start acting like you grown. Your mouth is too damn big. How many times do I have to tell you that? Now go get in that funky bedroom of yours. I need something to take the edge off." Smoke stood up from the table and looked at Chrystal, unfastening his belt as he motioned toward the bedroom.

"You ain't got to tell me shit! You must be crazy if you think I'm going to do anything with you. I swear it seems like y'all trying to set me up."

"Look here. You better get your shit together before I have to put a whipping on yo' ass. You think Duck pimp slapped you, just wait."

"Get your fat ass out of my house before I call the police. I'm through with y'all and all this nonsense. Get out now and don't come back with your old ass!" Chrystal was so mad that she was shaking, but she pulled her Glock from her waistband and pointed it at Smoke.

"Bitch, you crazy. You must don't know who you messing with. You pull a gun on somebody you better be ready to use it."

"You better believe I can use it, and I'm ready to blow a hole in your damn ass too." She released the safety and pointed the gun directly at Smoke's head.

Smoke threw up his hands and sarcastically said, "I'm through with your black ass. Nikki said you weren't worth it. You better remember what I said. You play too much. One day, you gonna fuck around with the wrong person. Here yo' damn money. Although you sure as hell didn't earn it." Chrystal made no move to take the money from Smoke.

"Just get the hell out of my house, you big fat turd, and I don't ever want to see you and your stank black ass again. And take your damn money with you. I don't want nothing from y'all. Give it to your ho, Nikki. I swear if she wasn't family, I would—"

"Yeah, right. We gonna see who come begging for this cheese before it's over, bitch." Smoke slowly backed up to the kitchen door. "Fuck you, bitch," he said. "Your pussy wasn't that good no way."

After Smoke left, Chrystal double-bolted the door and fell to the kitchen floor, crying and shaking like a leaf in a storm. She had just known this was going to be her last day on Earth, and she needed time to make so many things right. She had treated so many people wrong over the years, her mother being the first one on the list. She needed to come clean with her. She needed to talk to Jade's daddy. Hell she needed to talk to her own daddy because, until she did, she knew she would have no peace.

Twenty-four years ago

Eric and Jackie planned to meet at a hotel in College Park. They left work separately but agreed to meet at the Marriott. He was excited but disappointed all at the same time. He couldn't believe Jackie had actually asked him to help her make a baby. He knew how he felt about her, but it didn't seem she felt the same way. Sure, she liked him, but Eric wanted more. If it weren't for Lisa, things would have been so different. But if this was how she needed him, he would be more than happy to oblige.

He didn't know how he felt about babies and his part in it. Would she acknowledge him as the father, if it came to be, or was he to be just a sperm donor? Would he be allowed in the child's life? He didn't know how he felt about that either, but he was ready and able to do his part.

Eric had liked Jackie from the moment he met her. She was kind and passionate about her work. She really wanted to help people. When she was assigned as his human resources specialist to fill positions in customer service, he was ecstatic. She took her duties seriously. For a young woman, she had a lot of expertise. It really was a joy to work with her.

He remembered the first time he met her husband, Jimmy. The department held a holiday dinner at a popular restaurant. At the time, Jackie had only been married a few weeks, but Eric could tell that Jimmy wasn't the man for her. That fool spent most of his time sucking up to the VP instead of taking care of Jackie.

Eric thought that if it had been him, he would have skipped the dinner and been home getting dessert. It was more like Lisa should have been with Jimmy and Eric with Jackie. Besides, Jimmy gave off an air like he was so much better than Jackie, and Eric didn't care for that attitude at all.

If only she was his, if only he was free. Was it wrong? Should he be doing this? The answer was of course it was wrong and he shouldn't be doing it. But was it what he wanted? Yes, more than anything he wanted Jackie, and he wanted her to need him. And Eric knew that Jackie had captured his heart. He was now willing to do anything to keep her; even if it meant him telling her whatever she wanted to hear. Even if it wasn't the absolute truth.

Jackie was so scared that first time she met Eric at the hotel. If it hadn't been so important that she have a baby, she would have questioned her sanity. She loved her husband, right? *Then why are you out here, getting ready to do the nasty with another man? What if you get caught? You know people have been shot for less.* The little voice in her head just wouldn't let her be.

I'm doing this because *I do love my husband so much, and I know this is what our marriage needs. I know a baby would complete us. Oh Lord! I really do hope it's the right thing to do. I wouldn't do this if I had any other choice.* She told herself these things over and over. She said them so much that they became her mantra.

From the moment they met in the lobby, Eric's face lit up and he took the lead. He steered her to their room. He opened the door while never letting go of her hand. Jackie jokingly asked if he did this all the time because he was so good at it. He looked at her and shook his head no. "Nothing is too good for you, Jackie. You deserve this and so much more. I wish I could take you away for the weekend. But I want this to be special for you and me."

> *I see the answering look in your light brown eyes*
> *My heart leads me to confess that my very soul cries*
> *We made a big commitment; we both said yes, I do*
> *But with all my heart, I truly wish it had been to you*

She had been so nervous; it was a good thing they hadn't eaten first. She didn't think she would have been able to keep any food down. Her hands shook so badly that she couldn't remove her clothes. Eric had told her to let him. He was so gentle with her. He touched her as if she were a rare treasure he had unearthed. And as he removed each piece of clothing, he placed a gentle kiss on her heated flesh. He complimented her on her softness, her curves, her fragrant skin, her everything. She tried to cover herself with her hands, embarrassed by her imperfect body, but he took her hands away and kissed her fingertips. "Don't hide yourself from me," he said. "You're perfect in my eyes."

Eric kissed her lips then, and that one kiss contained all the passion he had longed to share with her. He looked at her with those sparkling eyes, and it sent her heartbeat into overdrive and hardened her nipples, almost painfully so. He caressed her breasts and tongued each one as if they were his personal caramel lollipops. He spread his palm over her slightly rounded stomach and reverently massaged the tension from her quivering belly. The lower he went the more excited and breathless she became. Everywhere he touched, he set her blood on fire and her mind couldn't—it just wouldn't—work. All she could do was whimper and pant. She had forgotten how to breathe. It felt so incredibly right, so wonderfully good.

And after he had hurriedly removed his clothes, she looked at him and marveled at how different he was from Jimmy. Where Jimmy was long and lean like a runner, Eric was muscled with hard abs and thick arms and legs. He had manly shoulders that you could lean on and trust that he could hold you up. Yes, this was it. This was so much better.

Eric easily cradled her in his strong arms and enfolded her in a sensual embrace that took over her senses. As he filled her with his essence, he murmured sweet words of passion, and she offered him all the love Jimmy didn't want. She kissed him over and over, demanding more with silent pleas. She ran her hands over him and marveled at his thickness, the power behind this man, all hard smooth flesh that burned even hotter at her caresses. She ran her fingers over every part of him and branded him as hers.

And Eric in return gave her everything, more than even she had imagined. His touch was electrifying, exhilarating, and her pulse beat erratically. There was no place he didn't kiss. Nothing was off limits, and she had never had any man treat her as if she were this special. He filled her as if he was made for her. She felt every pulse beat, every throb, and every inch of him. She was slick and wet with passion. She had never known it could be like this. This was the stuff of romance novels, but it was happening to her. All she could do was hold on and take what he was giving and pray it would never end. She cried then, the first real tears of joy she had ever experienced. Eric saw her tears and gently kissed each drop, and he smiled and told her that each tear only watered the love he had for her, so it could grow and grow.

Yet, that damn voice just kept on nagging her. *What are you doing? Are you crazy? This is not Jimmy. I know!* Jimmy had never done the things Eric was doing to her. *But this is for Jimmy. That's why I'm doing it, to make us a baby.*

But there was nothing clinical about what she was doing. This wasn't like a visit to the fertility clinic, where they injected you with a turkey baster. This was not an anonymous procedure, where you picked specimen number five out of the catalog. This was real, hot flesh and blood with a man who wasn't her husband. He was her lover.

Eric showed Jackie her first real glimpse of passion, and she didn't want it to stop. She was so greedy for more that she never wanted it to end. No matter what she tried to call it, Eric had moved her in ways that could never be undone.

The tension was still there at home, and she knew she had to get Jimmy to make love to her or all of it would have been for nothing. The minute he got back in town, she was on him. Sure, he complained. "Baby, let me unpack first. You can't be that happy to see me. I've only been gone for a couple of days."

"You're wrong, Jimmy. I missed you so much. I just want to show you how much. Come on. You can unpack later. I have something special to show you." And she tried her best to get Jimmy to comply, even holding the sexy lingerie she'd bought up to his face. He did seem to grow a little more interested and grabbed her hand, leading her to the bed.

But try as she might, she couldn't help but compare Jimmy to Eric. Jimmy was runway model lean while Eric was built like a warrior, all muscles and firm buttocks. Eric had thick arms and legs that picked her up and held her against the wall as they made love. She would have come closer to picking Jimmy up than he doing that to her. Where Eric took control and wanted her pleasure before his, Jimmy just lay back and expected her to get him ready. She didn't have to do all this with Eric. Eric was hard and ready just by taking off her clothes. She had to wear out her hand or mouth just to get a semi-erection out of Jimmy.

And that little voice in her head whispered, *See. Look what you've started. How are you going to do Jimmy when all you can think about is how wonderful it felt to be in Eric's arms? How he filled you completely, over and over again. How much you loved everything you did with him and begged him for more, just like the slut you are. You say it's for Jimmy, but who are you really kidding?*

To say being with Jimmy now was unfulfilling was way too kind, but she wanted to believe a baby would make Jimmy into the perfect husband. Then they would have the perfect marriage and together live happily ever after, but of course she was wrong.

She was being so careful, she thought, in her activities with Eric. No one at work suspected anything different between them. Eric treated her as usual, but he would linger a little longer when he touched her as he held the door open. His smile seemed brighter when he looked her way. She believed it didn't show on her face, but again she was so wrong.

What's the color of your tears?
Not one happy color of delight
Only mean dusty forgotten fears
Coming out to torment late at night

Saturday morning – the wedding day

Jackie pulled herself up out of the tangle of her bed covers. She had the worst hangover of her life. She'd thrown a pity party of one last night and had the splitting headache to prove it. Little dancing lights with fingers of acid pushed their way into her eyes. *I have got to stop drinking gin. It's definitely a killer.* She looked around her bedroom and noticed that she hadn't even turned the lights out last night. She also noticed the empty gin bottles tossed in the corner with her shoes. And her clothes were all over the place as if a fashion show had been going on and she'd tried on everything in her closet. She must not have enjoyed it because some of the clothes looked ripped apart and other pieces were turned inside out and balled up.

What in the hell have I done? She could remember taking a bath and crying herself silly over the sorry state of her life. She also remembered going to the kitchen and getting into her personal stash. What she didn't remember was drinking two bottles of gin. No wait, one of the bottles was tequila. She didn't even know she had tequila, but her stomach sure did now.

She sat up slowly and looked over at the clock. "What the hell? It's ten o'clock already." Her own loud voice made her ears ring. She flopped back down and winced as her head connected with the pillow. "Even the damn pillow hurts like hell."

She rubbed her eyes so hard she made her headache worse, and it felt like her fingers were going to push through to her brain. She stumbled as she finally made her way up and into the bathroom. She only had her bathrobe on, and it looked to be inside out. *I can't believe I left the bathroom like this.* Dingy, cold, gray water filled the bathtub, and her bath towels were a sodden mess on the floor, half in and half out of the bathtub.

Jackie almost screamed when she caught her reflection in the mirror. Her hair was all over her head. She usually double-strand twisted it at night with some of her creamed hair products, but now it looked like Jade had been playing in her hair. It was a tangled mess. And something that looked like carrots and peas was mixed in her hair. Her mouth tasted like muddy, shitty boots had been marching through it, and her teeth ached like somebody had stuck red hot pokers in her mouth.

What the hell was that scrawled on her mirror? Who had been in here writing shit all over the place? It looked like it read "'pitiful ho" and "sorri," or something like that, in lipstick. She must have been totally out of her mind to do that foolishness.

The biggest cramp in the world suddenly hit her square in the stomach. She barely made it to the toilet before all the foulness she had drunk the night before came gushing out.

Of course, she *would* hear the doorbell ringing over her hurling. Jackie was sweating and shaking so badly all she could do was sit on the floor and rest her head against the side of the commode. She heard someone come in and turn off the alarm, but at this point she just didn't care who it was.

"Jackie, what in the world is going on? I've been calling you all morning. Jackie! Oh my God, girl! What have you done to yourself?"

Nancy came into the bathroom and squatted down beside Jackie. She shook her head and tsk-tsked her. "You know better. What happened?"

"Nancy, is that you?" Jackie blubbered. "I don't know what I was thinking. I don't think I was thinking at all. My head's about to explode, and my stomach has already rebelled."

"I can smell that. Here, let me flush the toilet and get you up. You're a mess. Wipe your mouth. What were you drinking? It smells like burnt licorice and pigsty." Nancy steered Jackie over to the sink, took a washcloth, and wet it. She washed Jackie's face as if she were a small child.

"I came home last night, and it was so lonesome and quiet, and all I could do was think about what a terrible liar I am and a horrible person." Jackie started crying as if her heart was being ripped from her body. "I didn't want it to be like this. All I ever wanted was to have a happy marriage and beautiful babies and a man like daddy and . . ." The tears fell like a shimmering endless waterfall, wetting Jackie's face and dripping from her chin onto her chest.

"What are you talking about? You're not a liar. You're my wonderful baby sister, and I love you. Why didn't you call me? I would have come over and shared a drink or two with you, not drink the entire liquor store like you did." Nancy cupped Jackie's face and continued to wipe at the tears. "Besides, you know I'm here for you, just like you've always been for me."

Jackie continued to cry and whimper like a lost child.

"What's really the problem? What happened last night to make you like this? And what is this shit written on the mirror? And what is this in your hair?" Nancy wiped her hand on Jackie's robe after she lifted what looked like cheese from Jackie's hair.

"You just don't know me. I'm a liar and a slut. I've done things that would make you hate me. I lied to everybody about Chrystal and Royce's daddy. I even lied to the daddy. I messed up so many people's lives. Nobody wants me. Nobody loves me. I'm not worthy of love." Jackie slumped to the floor in defeat.

"Look at me. Stop this! If you lied to Jimmy, then good. He deserved it. I never liked his crazy ass anyway. Get yourself together. You have a wedding to go to. You're the mother of the groom. I don't know what you're talking about, but whatever happened, you had a good reason. I know you're loved by so many people. I love you, Jackie. You're my little sister. You are not only my sister but my best friend, so I need you to stop beating yourself up. Now get up off this floor and get into that shower. You smell like Jade's diapers."

"No, not cheating-ass Jimmy. I mean Eric. I lied to him about how I felt. I didn't do right by him. I used him, just like Jimmy used me. Once I had too many men, and now I don't have any. Oh God, Nancy! I deserve everything I'm getting now."

Nancy tried her best to clean Jackie up, but her sister's comments stopped her in her tracks. "What do you mean Eric? You mean that good looking guy you used to work with. I always thought you talked a lot about him. I used to wonder what happened to him. He sure seemed to be a better man than Jimmy. I can't really blame you for that."

Nancy continued to pull discarded food out of Jackie's hair. "Now you know I was only supposed to come over and help you get ready for the wedding. But now it looks like I'm going to have to do a complete makeover to get you presentable. And dropping Eric's name like that is giving me too much to think about. Not Jimmy, uh, but Eric. Well I'll be. Like I said lil sister, I can't blame you for that."

Nancy ushered her sister into the shower and turned on the water. "Jackie, you have got to help me. Now I know you can wash yourself. I'm not going to touch all your titties and stuff. Here. Use this shampoo on your hair. Why do you have food in there anyway? What in God's name were you doing?" Nancy squeezed more shampoo onto Jackie's hair while trying not to get wet by the shower.

Jackie knew she had said too much but her head was killing her and she couldn't think clearly. Now Nancy knew more than she meant to tell her. But what the hell; it was about time to be honest with her. "I don't remember much, but I think I got hungry with all the drinking and made myself something to eat. Everything is kind of hazy now. Lord, my hair is so messed up. I'm never going to get it right in time. I can't seem to do anything right. I just keep messing up everything, everybody's life. Oh Lord, Nancy!"

"Look, you have got to stop all this crying. I've seen enough of your snot. I'll get you ready if it's the last thing I do. Now rinse that shampoo out of your hair and get your fat butt in gear. I'm going to make us some coffee and get you some toast. When I come back, I want to see you sitting on that stool, ready for me to start on your hair. This is going to take some doing."

Nancy followed the trail of dirty dishes and dried food back to the kitchen. It looked like her old second grade class had been there trying to cook. She wasn't sure, but something that looked like cheese was burned onto the stovetop. And peas and carrots were all over the floor, along with a box of macaroni noodles. *What was she trying to do, make macaroni and cheese? I'll just have to clean this mess up later. I just can't get over the Eric thing. I never thought about it but I did kind of suspect their marriage breakup involved a third party,* thought Nancy as she hurried over to the sink.

It was already eleven o'clock, and they were supposed to get to Ms. Sylvi's house by noon. There was no way they were going to make that time.

Royce came through the kitchen door from the garage and gave his aunt a kiss and a hug. "Hey, Aunt Nancy. How you doing? What in the world happened to the kitchen?"

"Hey, baby. Your mother happened to the kitchen. She decided she wanted to celebrate your wedding a little early and all by herself. She's in her bathroom, but Royce, don't say anything. She's really hungover and taking you getting married pretty hard. Just leave her alone for a while, and she'll be all right."

Royce spoke rather loudly. "But Aunt Nancy, we've had this talk. I don't know why she feels this way. I'm a grown man, and I have a right to make my own decisions."

"Shh! I know all that, but she just needs time. Okay? Besides, you look like you've been out having too much fun too!" Nancy set the carafe on the coffeemaker to brew. "If I didn't know better, I'd say that look on your face seems like you've seen too many clear-heeled shoes. Am I right?"

"Well, the guys just wanted to take me out for one last blow out. Anyway, I'm going to get cleaned up and get ready to jump the broom." Royce gave his aunt another hug and whispered, "Take care of Mom. I know it's difficult for her, and I love her more than anything, but I've got to live my own life."

"I know, Royce. I truly do. Now, go on. I need to get some bread in your mother's stomach to soak up all that alcohol. I'll handle it. Don't worry. Don't worry about anything."

Nancy was true to her word, but it was almost one o'clock when they pulled up to their mother's house in the van Nancy had rented to take everyone to the wedding.

Nancy thought Jackie's hair really was amazing. Her natural hair was curly and had just the right texture. It fell around her face, highlighting her eyes. She looked much younger than her forty-nine years. The lime green dress she had on fit her body like a glove, accentuating every curve.

Jackie took her time getting out of the van since she was still nursing a splitting headache. She hadn't said two words to Nancy on the drive over. She felt like all kinds of fools and was worried that she may have said too much earlier. "Nancy, don't say anything to Mom about, you know, what I did. I feel so foolish now. I mean, I don't know what I mean. Can you tell? I feel like it must be written all over my face. My head sure feels like shit."

"Jackie, you worry too much. You look great. Mom called a few times, but I said you had a stomachache. That's all. We still have plenty of time. Look who's running out to greet us."

"Grandma Jack! Look at me. Granny got me a balloon and some candy, and she let me sleep with her and she, she . . ." Jewel was so happy to see Jackie that she danced and hopped all around her. "I got candy and a new dress to wear to Uncle Royce wedding and everything. And I'm going to carry the flowers and throw them down and look pretty too."

Jackie rubbed her forehead and slowly said, "I know you are, honey. I have your dress right here. Let's go in the house and see what Granny's doing, okay?" Jackie made no move towards the house so Nancy pushed Jackie forward. She had to lead not only Jewel but a reluctant Jackie back to the house.

"Okay, Mom. Let me finish this last curl in your hair. You look beautiful, just like a bride yourself," said Nancy as she finished curling her mother's hair. Everyone was dressed in various shades of green. Nancy had come up with the idea, and Jackie helped her put it into motion. Ms. Sylvi's outfit was a pale green two-piece suit with a beautiful multicolored broach pinned to the lapel. Buddy had given the broach to her years ago for their forty-fifth wedding anniversary.

Ms. Sylvi was sitting on the vanity bench looking in the mirror. "Nancy, you know you lying. I'm way too old to be looking like anybody's bride, but Jackie sure does look pretty. In fact, you all are just so beautiful. Just like a beautiful flower garden." Warm golden tears suddenly shone in Ms. Sylvi's eyes. "I wish Buddy was here to see this day. I can't believe my only grandson is getting married today. I remember when he was born. All that reddish hair. Looked just like you, Jackie. I always thought he did."

"Well, Mom, I guess so." Jackie squirmed in her reclining position up against the bathroom door. They were all in their mother's bathroom doing hair just like when they were teenagers, except Jackie could only think about how messed up her life was. Long gone were the days when she saw a bright future for herself and just knew her Prince Charming was waiting out there somewhere for her.

"Hey, where everybody at? I got Oro and Jade all ready." Chrystal came through the bedroom and stood in the bathroom door with Jade on her hip and Oro holding her hand. "Chantrelle and her mom just dropped us off. They said they'd see us at the wedding."

"Hand that little Jade to Granny, so I can get some sugar. How you, Miss Jade? You sure do look pretty with all these pretty green ribbons in your hair."

Jade laughed and giggled at her great-grandmother and went willingly into her arms.

"Chrystal, you look beautiful. You look like you should be getting married today. That dress is just right, not too tight, not too short, just right." Ms. Sylvi held Jade and looked Chrystal over. "What's that on your face there. You got a bruise?"

"Oh yeah, Grandma. I fell up against the refrigerator last night, but it's okay. I thought I had covered it over pretty good."

"Well, it is covered real good, but I know how you really look, and there's just a little bit too much makeup right there. Anyway, don't she look beautiful? And look at little man here. He's so handsome. Come here, Oro, and give Granny a kiss."

Chrystal nudged a laughing Oro over to his great-grandmother and turned to look at Jackie. "Hi, Mom. You look so pretty. That dress really fits great. Just like Grandma said, not too tight, not too short, just right." Everybody had to laugh at the silliness, and it took a great amount of tension out of the room.

Jewel twirled around in her new dress and asked, "What about me, Mommy? Am I pretty too? I had candy and a balloon and got to sleep with Granny."

Chrystal held her arms out to Jewel and said, "Of course you are, baby. Come give me a kiss. I missed all of you guys so much. And Aunt Nancy you look great too. That pants outfit is just right for you. That green shade looks great with your silver hair. I got my cell phone. Let's take a picture. But not in here, let's go into the living room. Y'all know I'm the selfie queen. This is going to be so great. All the women in the family in one room, and we are looking so fabulous."

"Don't forget about little man here with his little suit and that long black hair, which needs to be cut. How did you even find something in this green shade for a toddler?" Nancy asked as she bent to lift him up off the floor.

"Mom found it, didn't you, Mama? She knew exactly where to get all the kids' outfits. They fit perfectly. She even picked this dress out for me and the shoes too." It was a sleeveless lime green sheath dress with just a touch of contrast piping around the V-neck and the shoes were red Aldo's Jackie had found on sale. "I thought at first that it wasn't going to fit me right and would make me look too old, but I was wrong. It's beautiful. Thank you, Mama." Chrystal spun around so that everyone could get a perfect view.

Jackie couldn't believe her ears. Was this her Chrystal saying these things? Chrystal had never given her a compliment or thanked her for as long as she could remember. She wondered, *what in the world happened to her after she left the rehearsal?*

"You're welcome, baby. I knew it would flatter your complexion, and with your figure, an old sack would look gorgeous on you." Jackie led everyone out of the bedroom. "You know, Mom. I think we need somebody to take a picture of all of us together. Do you know if Mr. Turner is at home? I bet he would come over and take a picture. Nancy, did you bring your camera?"

"Sure did. Got my Canon in the van. I think you're right, Jackie. We need a group picture. Let me go get the camera and see if Mr. Turner's home. While I'm gone, y'all can practice with Miss Selfie Queen here." Before Nancy left the living room she handed Oro over to Crystal and asked, "by the way Chrystal, I always meant to ask about the children's names. They really are unique and I always wondered about that. There seems to be a pattern; Jewel, Oro and Jade, but I just can't put it all together."

Chrystal looked around the living room at her closest family members and sighed. "Well, I really didn't have a theme in mind, if that's what you mean. I just wanted my baby to have a name of worth. I guess I always felt my name represented something fragile and easily broken. When it cracks and breaks there will be nothing left but worthless glass."

Nancy gasped and said, "Chrystal you can't mean that."

Chrystal looked at Jackie and stammered, "Well, I don't think it was intentional on mom and daddy's part. At least I hope not, but that's just how I felt. So when Jewel was born, I wanted to name her something valuable, something priceless you know. A precious Jewel."

Ms. Sylvi teared up and said, "Chrystal, baby you know that's not true. You know your mother named you something lovely. A beautiful natural piece of the world and . . ."

"Well grandma that's how you see it but I didn't. So when Oro was born I named him something priceless too. Because Oro means gold in

Spanish. You know people have always searched the world over for gold. He's my golden boy and he'll always know he means so much to me."

"And Jade's name?" said Nancy.

"Jade's name is something that is distinctive also. Jade represents wisdom and good fortunate in so many cultures. I wanted my kids to at least have a name that represented something respected and valuable, that had a positive meaning."

Everyone was stunned into silence after Chrystal's confession. Blue tears filled Jackie's eyes and she saw before her a Chrystal she never knew existed. "Chrystal, I don't know what to say. I didn't name you for a worthless piece of glass. When your father and I looked at you, we just knew that you were a wonder of nature. A perfect design; your eyes were like beautiful sparkling crystals. It was not a slight; it was a beautiful name for our precious baby girl." Jackie lowered her head and slowly walked out the front door. Chrystal had given her too much to think about.

They all stood outside, right in front of the roses. Mr. Turner had gladly come over to get in their business and take the picture. "Y'all some good-looking women. Where everybody going so dressed up? Sylvi, I ain't seen you this pretty in years. You look just like you used to before Buddy passed. Let me see. Where my glasses? These new cameras ain't what I'm used to."

"Just take the pictures, Frank, and don't worry about where we going," said Ms. Sylvi rather rudely.

"Mama, you didn't tell Mr. Turner about Royce getting married today?" Nancy asked. She wondered what had been going on between her mother and Mr. Turner for Ms. Sylvi to react so negatively. She had never seen her mother be this rude to him before and they had been neighbors for over forty years.

Ms. Sylvi just looked at Nancy and motioned for her to hush.

Chrystal and Jackie were trying so hard not to laugh but couldn't hold back, especially after Mr. Turner turned a pitiful look their way. "I guess I'll just take my old self back to the house. All I'm good for is to take a picture. Not to be invited to the wedding even. What kind of neighbor are you, Sylvi?"

Ms. Sylvi harrumphed. "It's time to go. Get all those baby seats in the van. We just wasting time, standing out here talking to this old man."

"Mama, that's so rude," said Nancy as she took her camera back from Mr. Turner. "Thank you, Mr. Turner, and I'm so sorry. We must have missed getting you an invitation. I don't know what has come over our mother, but I apologize for her."

"That's all right, Nancy. I know who I'm dealing with. Y'all have a good wedding, and give my best wishes to Royce and his bride. Y'all be safe now."

Nancy just shook her head at Ms. Sylvi and Mr. Turner. *I bet there's a lot more going on here than they are letting on,* she thought to herself. *I'll have to ask Jackie later if she had noticed anything.*

8

What's the color of your tears?
Dripping like muddy raindrops
Ultimate betrayer, flaunting fears
Purple-tipped cascade never stops

Saturday afternoon – the wedding chapel

Everyone was excited as Nancy maneuvered the van into the Faithful Dove's parking lot. It was 2:45, and the lot was already full. They pulled into a handicapped space and unloaded.

"I'm so glad we made it. After that traffic accident on the Stone Mountain Freeway, I thought that was it," said Nancy as she helped her mother out of the van.

"So did I, and I wasn't even driving," said Jackie as she slipped her Louboutins on and shoved her slippers under the seat. "Okay. We're ready to do this, right?"

A chorus of YES! filled the air. They all marched into the hall as if they were a force to be reckoned with. One of the ushers stopped them and asked, "Friends of the bride or groom?"

Jackie shot the poor man a look that would have melted stone. "I'm the groom's mother, and this is the rest of his immediate family. Didn't anybody tell you that? My granddaughter is the flower girl. Please escort her to where she should go." Jackie snapped at the poor man until he was stammering and stuttering.

"I-I'm sorry, Mrs. Mattock. I was filling in for one, for one of the Faithful Dove's regular ushers. Please proceed to your seats, and I will personally take the flower girl to the rest of the wedding party in Room A."

"You tell him, Mama. He must not know who he messing with. That's my mama, fool." Chrystal was being so silly that everyone laughed and proceeded to their seats. A multitude of white and blush roses and rosebuds decorated the hall. They covered almost every surface, including the altar, and big bouquets of ribbons and roses decorated the ends of each row of seats. It was beautiful and smelled wonderful.

Jackie nodded as she passed several friends and neighbors who they had invited. Her cousin Sheila was there with her third husband. Jackie couldn't even remember his name. *I think it's Ralph or something.* And there were Clara and Chantrelle and Christian. *Chantrelle even has her boyfriend with them. There's Aunt Anita, Uncle Henry, and so many others.* She smiled as she passed everyone, making her way to her seat.

She saw Tony Baldwin from work seated on their side of the aisle and gave him a bright smile and a wink. *I think it's time to give him a chance,* she thought as she took her seat. *It's time for me to let go of the past and start making a real life for myself. Enough of the pity party already, time for a new beginning.*

She nodded to Natalie Reese, who was already seated. Natalie looked like she'd just stepped off the page of a bridal magazine cover. Didn't the woman know no one is to upstage the bride, least of all the bride's mother? That's why all those bridesmaids' dresses were so hideous. But Natalie had on a shimmering dusty rose outfit that fit her to a T. She was all smiles while she wrung her hands together in a death grip. A woman who looked very similar to her sat beside her. *That must be the sister I've heard about.* She looked just like Natalie but taller. She was also dressed to kill. Jackie noticed several others of Natalie and Earl's family members, including Earl's mother. She had met some of them before, but gathered here together, they were a beautiful family.

Wow! Natalie sure looks nervous, thought Jackie as she pulled a sniffling Jade closer to her side. "What's the matter with Grandma's little cutie? Chrystal, she feels kind of warm. Make sure to give her some Pedialyte when you get home." Out of the corner of her eye, Jackie saw two men come down the aisle. She turned her head slightly to get a better look.

Oh my God. Jimmy and Bryan. Oh no, oh no, oh hell no! I just knew Royce was going to do something stupid like this and invite Jimmy. Of all the people she didn't want to see today, Jimmy and Bryan were tops on the list. *Just look at them*, she thought. *Jimmy has the nerve to walk in here and bring his little boyfriend on top of everything else. After how many years? And he doesn't look like he's aged one bit. I don't even see a gray hair in his perfect haircut. He's still lean and dressed like a runway model. Now Bryan does look like he's seen better times. Is that a beer gut on him? And that hair, that is one bad dye job. Yes, there is a Jesus! Just wait till this wedding is over. Oh Lordy, just wait.*

Thankfully the wedding march started before Jackie could get up and make a total fool of herself. Royce and his best man stood at the altar. Royce looked regal in his wedding clothes. The dove gray color brought out the light already shining in his eyes. He looked so happy.

Everyone stood and turned to the back as the bridesmaids took their walk down the aisle with the groomsmen. They were indeed beautiful people, even with hideous tapioca-colored dresses and matching cummerbunds. The music was superb and added just the right touch to the nuptials. Jackie had been a little skeptical when Royce and Jessica said they wanted something different played, but the old school Peaches and Herb tunes were lovely.

"Oh my, look at Jewel," said Jackie. The little girl came down the aisle tossing out flowers as if she had practiced all day. She was such a little cutie. She stopped at her mother's seat and asked, "Is this right, Mommy? Am I doing good?" Everyone laughed as Chrystal said, "Yes, baby, you're doing just right."

Then, in came Jessica. She was radiant in an antique wedding dress full of lace. The train was spectacular and trailed behind her like a river. Her veil covered her face, but everyone could see how beautiful she was on her wedding day. As the wedding march concluded at the rose covered altar, Earl proudly presented her.

"You may be seated," said the minister. "Dearly beloved, we are gathered here today to bind Jessica Joy Reese and Royce Clayton Mattock in holy matrimony. Who gives this woman to this man?"

"Her mother and I give our daughter Jessica Joy Reese to Royce Clayton Mattock," said Earl as he nervously stepped back and took a seat beside Natalie. Natalie's eyes were filling with tears even as Earl hugged her close.

Jackie tuned out most of what the minister was saying. She was too busy looking around to see who had shown up. She whispered, "Chrystal, who's that man sitting with your cousin Nikki back there?"

"What man? Who are you talking about?" Chrystal whispered and then took a swift look back where her mother had indicated. "That's Smoke. The guy I told you about doing the videos with."

Ms. Sylvi had enough and whispered to both of them to hush up. Then she gave them both the side eye. "Y'all messing this up with all your talking."

"Jessica and Royce wanted to share the vows they wrote with everyone. Go ahead, Jessica," said Reverend Benson as he stepped back behind the couple.

"Royce, you studied quantum mechanics
I studied the poetry of mid-century authors
You understood it as the physics of pure thought
I felt it from the soul's deep delight

Together as one, we came into being
A quark in the maelstrom of time
Physics to me was magic
Something I couldn't explain or understand

Poetry to you was nonsense
Something you didn't have time to hear
Musings by long dead authors

Together, unspoken, we understood both
And knew we had fallen in love
Royce, I give myself to you."

Everyone clapped as Jessica finished. "I don't know what she was talking about, but it sure does sound pretty," said Ms. Sylvi as she wiped tears of happiness from her eyes.

"And now Royce, would you please share your vows."

"Jessica, I will love and respect myself for you
I will defend your honor to the last for you
Flip off the rest of the world for you
Honor you till the day I die, for you

With all that GOD has put in me for you
I will gladly be the lover for you
With every beat of my heart for you
I will love you till the day I die, for you

I will breathe my last breath for you
I will stand tall and sturdy for you
I will and can live for you

Because I could do no less for you
Jessica, I give myself to you."

Everyone clapped so loud and so long that Reverend Benson just stood behind Jessica and Royce and held his hands over their heads. The love in that room was being freely shared; it was contagious. It made the older people remember when and why they fell in love, and the youngsters fervently prayed that kind of love would one day come their way.

"Oh, Jackie, that was so wonderful. I've never heard such beautiful sentiments," said Nancy as she wiped at her eyes again. "It makes you wish for someone to hold late at night who feels that way about you. And the refrain of 'for you' was just so clever. I didn't know Royce wrote. He's so talented." Nancy continued whispering her sentiments, but Jackie had stopped listening to her.

She sat ramrod straight and stared at Royce and Jessica. *That's the poetry I wrote*, she thought. *How did Royce get it? I'll be damned. And there he stands, smiling at me like I gave it to him. The only way he could have gotten it was if he broke into my laptop. I know I've never been that careless to leave it open. I don't think I did. Oh Lord! I don't know now what I did. All I do know is that my son is way more devious than I ever knew.*

"I now pronounce Jessica and Royce husband and wife. Royce, you may kiss your beautiful bride." The audience whooped and clapped so loudly as Royce kissed Jessica that no one noticed the look on Jackie's face.

She was the proverbial angry black woman, but even more so, she was saddened by the actions of her son. *I've given him everything I could, and he sneaks behind my back and uses my innermost feelings and heartaches as if they were his own.* She felt so violated. *He could have asked me to help him write something. I would have gladly given him these words, but no, he somehow found them and used them. Look at Natalie and Earl looking at the happy couple like Royce is a gift from heaven. And my family too. Nancy can't say enough wonderful things about his vows. Even Chrystal has a tear in her eye.*

Royce finally finished kissing Jessica and looked at his mother. He blew her a kiss as if she was in on this. *So this is what Earl was talking about when he asked about a special surprise. The nerve of Royce! I can't believe my own son would do this to me.*

People were congratulating Royce and Jessica on their new marriage. Not wanting to miss out on the sumptuous gourmet buffet and open bar, most folks were on their way to Room B, where Reverend Benson had announced the reception would be held. Jackie sat still in her seat. Chrystal and the kids had to squeeze around her to get out.

"Jackie, what is wrong with you? Why haven't you moved?" Before Jackie could answer Nancy, she continued. "I've never seen or heard such a beautiful ceremony. From the decorations and music right down to their own vows they wrote, everything was so unique and special."

"Royce didn't write that. He stole that." Jackie finally moved and let Nancy pass. Nancy gave her a look but didn't say anything. Ms. Sylvi was already heading to the reception and hadn't noticed Jackie hanging back. Nancy rushed to catch up to her mother.

Jackie looked around, still in a state of shock, and saw Jimmy and Bryan headed her way. From the opposite direction, Tony was coming over and reached her first.

"Hi, Tony. I'm so glad you made it," Jackie said as she smiled at him. "That suit looks fantastic on you. How many phone numbers have you gotten so far?" She saw Jimmy and Bryan hang back as she spoke to Tony.

Tony gave Jackie a kiss and a big hug. "Jackie, you are the most beautiful woman here, beside the bride of course. The only phone number I'm interested in is yours, and I already have it. By the way, the ceremony was fantastic. I know you're so proud. I see there are some people waiting to speak to you, so I'll see you at the buffet."

"Okay, Tony. I'll talk to you in a minute." Jackie saw Jimmy and Bryan continue her way. Royce's betrayal had taken most but not all of the fight out of her, so she barely nodded to Jimmy as he said hello.

"Well, Jackie, how have you been?" said a smiling Jimmy. "I see you're as popular as ever. You look great by the way. I felt so special when Royce called me and personally invited us to the wedding."

Bryan came over and stood closer to Jimmy, and Jimmy said, "You know it's been a while since we've spoken, Jackie, but I want you to know that I feel the past is just that. Let's keep it there and focus on the future. Starting here today, I want to celebrate love and life. I've come to realize that we don't get do-overs, but we can learn from our mistakes and move forward."

Either they didn't notice the death wish in Jackie's eyes, or they were too full of themselves to feel the hatred coming off Jackie in waves.

"Those sure are lovely and insightful words, especially coming from you, Jimmy. I didn't know you had it in you to be this magnanimous. Is this part of your master plan also? Take the high road, be the bigger person?" Jackie practically spit the words at the couple.

Jackie gave Bryan the once-over and sarcastically said, "Bryan, I see you're looking well. What are you now, sixty-five, seventy? You're holding together remarkably well for someone your age. It must be difficult with all the wear and tear Jimmy must put on you."

Bryan turned red at Jackie's comments and didn't answer. Jimmy looked at Jackie, shaking his head, and said, "You know that wasn't called for. I try to bury the hatchet, and you just want to start some bullshit. Why is it always this way between—"

"Stop right there." Jackie shook her finger in Jimmy's face. "If I remember correctly, the last one of us who tried to 'bury the hatchet,' as you say, was me. I called you about Chrystal, and you buried the hatchet in my back, as usual. I really don't want to listen to anything you have to say."

An idea suddenly hit her. "Go tell your grandchildren all that mess since you haven't ever met them. I didn't invite you here, and I don't need you here. Apparently you've been communicating with Royce, so you can just keep on doing that. Right now, I don't want to have anything to do with you or your senior citizen boyfriend." Jackie turned on her heel and, as calmly as possible, walked to the reception room.

Chrystal went to find Nikki and Smoke. *What's this bitch trying to prove?* She knew he wasn't invited. If it hadn't looked funny, she would have uninvited Nikki too, after the shit she pulled. *Look at them over there, looking like a fat bull and a fat cow. I don't believe this sow got the nerve to grin at me too. And look at Smoke, cheesing like he just got fed. I can't stand neither one of them. The nerve of that bitch!*

"Hey, Nikki. Let me talk to you a minute. I see you made it to the wedding. By the way, I don't remember sending an invitation to you, Calvin. Just why are you here?"

Chrystal looked at Nikki and Smoke as if they were something to be scraped off the bottom of her shoes. *They couldn't look more ghetto if they tried.* Smoke was so played out in that lab-coat-looking suit he had on. It looked grimy and smelled worst. She didn't know they still made mess like that. The tight, short shit that Nikki wore looked like it came straight from the dollar store and every seam was screaming to be let go. Her titties were pushed up so high they bounced against her chin with every step she took. If she bent over half an inch, all her fat ass would be hanging out. And that pink yarn in her braids was so old that it looked worse than a moldy rag left out in the rain.

"I would have thought you were recuperating after last night, Calvin," said Chrystal in a sugary sweet voice. "Oh, my bad! I'm the one who should be recuperating, considering I was beat up by your no good friends."

"Chrystal, you're always the drama queen," said Nikki as she gave Chrystal the side eye. "Didn't nobody beat you up. From what Calvin said, Duck barely touched you. I don't even see a scratch on you. You're just making shit up as usual."

Nikki grabbed a reluctant Calvin's arm, stumbling up against him in her too tall heels. "Besides, Calvin is my escort, and the invitation didn't say I couldn't bring a guest. Anyway, you need to handle your business better. You never know what ugly gossip Cousin Jackie might have heard about you and your activities." Nikki said this sweetly as she held tightly to Calvin's arm to keep from falling over.

Smoke or Calvin tried to jump in the conversation as if he were an invited guest. "Yeah, Chrystal, what I tell you? You always talk too much. I told you to respect grown folks. Now get out of our way so we can congratulate the happy couple." Smoke and Nikki tried to push past Chrystal, but she didn't budge.

Chrystal lowered her voice and said, "Look here, bitches. Don't make me get ugly here at my brother's wedding. You and Smoke know damn well what happened last night. Now you both got the nerve to show up here and act like I did something stupid." Chrystal noticed people were starting to look their way. She didn't want to show out at Royce's wedding, so she toned it down some more.

"Look, I got too much respect for my real family to get into some mess with y'all. I don't know what gossip you're talking about, but let me warn you. I'm not going to play games with you, Nikki, and certainly not you, Smoke. I am through with you both, and I mean what I say, and I'm ready to back it up. Don't be causing no shit up in here. Get your little feed on—like either one of you need more food—then you both get the hell out of here and out of my life."

Chrystal turned her back on them both and went over to where her grandmother, aunt, and kids waited in the receiving line. One thing she knew for sure was that, as of last night, she was through with the lowlife, bullshit people she had been associating with.

Jackie stood silently by the receiving line. Everyone was so happy with big grins radiating from their faces. Her joy had been stolen by her own son. She finally stood in front of Royce and Jessica and pulled Royce close for a hug. Quietly, only for his ears, she said, "I don't know what game you're playing, but I'm not happy with it. How did you get my poetry? Those were my private papers. I just knew something terrible was going to happen today, but I never thought you'd be responsible for it."

"Mom, what are you talking about? I thought you'd be so happy if I used your writing. When I asked you about writing something for the wedding, you said, 'Sure, Royce.' And then you left your computer on with this poem open, so I thought it was what you wanted me to use. I didn't know you'd be upset." Royce stepped back out of his mother's arms and put his arm around Jessica. She was looking at the scene in front of her with concern on her face.

"Mama Jackie, is everything okay? The poetry you wrote for Royce was so beautiful. I just want to thank you again. Mine was all right, but you have such talent. I knew I should have asked you to write mine also."

Jackie knew she was holding up the line, but she didn't care. What was wrong with her? She didn't remember Royce asking her for any poetry. She felt like the biggest fool. "Okay, Royce. I must have forgotten. I'm sorry. I didn't mean to accuse you of something you didn't do, but you did invite your father without my knowledge. You should have told me so I could have prepared myself better. It was a bit of a shock to see him here, especially with Bryan."

Jackie stepped back a little and said. "Anyway, I'm going to get out of the way and let the rest of these people congratulate you and Jessica. Oh, and thank you, Jessica, for liking my poetry. Just let me know anytime you need some inspirational writing." Jackie tried to smile as she walked away, but her heart just wasn't in it.

~∾

Nikki stopped Jackie and wouldn't let her pass. "Cousin Jackie, everything is so beautiful. The color of the bridesmaids' dresses is gorgeous. And that old-school music is just right for them. Royce always was kind of old timey. Anyway, I know you're so proud of Royce, what with his great job and now he's gotten married. And the bride don't even have a bunch of kids already."

Jackie was sick of everything and everybody. She tried to move on, but Nikki rambled on and on. "This is my fiancé, Calvin. I hope one day to have a beautiful wedding like this. Minus the old-school music though, 'cause I just can't get to that. I would just love to march down the aisle to some Jay-Z. Anyway, I know you probably wish Chrystal was getting married too. But that probably won't happen with all the kids she has. She just can't seem to find one man who's willing to settle down with her. You know with all the baby-daddies and what not. Isn't that right, Calvin?"

Jackie looked at the man Nikki held on to so tightly. She thought, *if this is the best you can do, then I feel sorry for you.* This man was certainly no prize. Nikki wasn't much older than Chrystal, but this Calvin person looked to be about forty with a pot belly. Those dreads were so nasty looking that Jackie expected something to crawl out of them any minute now. And what in heaven's name was that smell? Was it his breath? Oh Lord! It was a cross between corn chips, old cheese, and something even more foul. Both of them looked like a hot mess ten times over. And why all the digs about Chrystal? Suddenly a voice started playing back in her head. All the crazy phone calls, that voice sounded a lot like Nikki here.

Jackie wanted so badly to call bullshit on them but she wanted to play with them a little before she dismissed them. "Thanks, Nikki, and congratulations to you both on your engagement. You two make the perfect couple. I know Sheila must be proud of you also. What is it you're doing now? The Quickie Mart, right? And Calvin looks like such wonderful husband material. Chrystal told me you produced something. Is that right, Calvin?"

"Yes, ma'am. Something like that. Come on, Nikki. Let's get something to eat before we leave," mumbled Calvin as he scratched his head.

"Oh, don't be so formal, Calvin. You can call me Jackie since we're about the same age. Oh, and don't forget to give your gift to one of the ushers. Thanks for coming. I know it means so much to Royce and Jessica."

"Okay, Cousin Jackie, you take care, and we'll see you later." Nikki and Calvin gave her a funny look, but what the hell? She didn't care. Somebody needed to set Nikki straight. *The nerve of that little bitch. Who in hell does she think she's fooling? I hope Chrystal has realized what these fools are trying to do to her. And Nikki is family too. What a piece of nothing that Calvin person is. I wouldn't let him sleep in my backyard, much less let him in the house.* And of course they hadn't brought anything but she wanted them to know she knew that.

Jackie saw Jimmy and Bryan heading over to Chrystal and the kids. *Now, here's where the fun comes in. I just can't wait until Chrystal chews his ass out and that prissy Bryan holding on to him like a love-sick woman too. I should get the camera from Nancy just to take a picture of his face when she tells him off. Just because Royce made up with him doesn't mean Chrystal has.*

"Grandpa Jimmy!" yelled a giggling Jewel. "Did you see me throw down the flowers? Mama said I did real good, and I'm getting some cake, and Jade is getting cake, but Oro can't have any cake because he wet himself and—"

"Yes, baby, I saw you with the flowers, and you did a wonderful job. Come give Grandpa a big hug, and you too, Oro. Did you wet yourself again? Bryan get my little Jade so I can give her a big kiss too."

Ms. Sylvi even got in on the act. "Jimmy, oh my Lord! It has been way too long. You still handsome though. I'm so glad you made it to see my Royce get married. My grandson is so handsome. He got himself a beautiful bride too. Oh my! It is just so good to see you."

Jimmy gave Ms. Sylvi a hug and whispered something that Jackie couldn't make out. Ms. Sylvi blushed and tapped him on his shoulder. Jackie was amazed by the domestic scene of happiness going on around her. She couldn't have been more bewildered if Reverend Benson had stood up and said he himself was marrying Jessica instead of Royce. It looked again like she was the one who didn't have a clue. She was the one who had been left out. She thought she held all the cards, all the secrets, but she was the one left holding the losing hand.

What the hell was going on? The kids were hanging all over Jimmy and Bryan as if they knew them. Chrystal had her arm through Jimmy's like he was really a father to her. *What has been going on behind my back?* This was too much. She knew she was still hungover from last night, but not to the point where she was imagining things. Chrystal and the kids were hugging Jimmy and Bryan like they had a current, happy relationship, and they must have for Jewel to know who they were. Even her mother hung on every word Jimmy uttered.

Jackie felt big scarlet tears threatening to escape. Her eyes were hot and blurry, and her head was starting to pound all over again. Why was she the last to know what her family was doing with her ex? How could they do this to her? She felt so betrayed.

"Jackie, what's going on?" Nancy asked. "I didn't expect Jimmy to be here. I see he's still hanging with that Bryan guy. When did Chrystal and the kids start seeing him?"

Jackie could scarcely talk, she was so disheartened, but she somehow found the words to answer Nancy. "I didn't expect this either. Apparently, I'm the last one to know what's going on under my own roof. Today has just been full of surprises. I don't think I can handle any more. In fact, I think I need to go somewhere and sit down. I suddenly feel really overheated and sick to my stomach."

"There's a lounge over there. Let's go in there and cool off. You really do look like you're going to be sick. This green isn't helping any. Your face is starting to look the same color. Let me get you settled, and then I'll get your friend Tony to look after you. He was just looking for you." Nancy steered Jackie to the back room, all the while, the wedding party and guests laughed, having a wonderful time. Just like one big happy family.

How could she have heard, but didn't hear? And surely she had seen, but she still didn't see.

I created a monster
From such a tiny little thing
I fed it 'til it couldn't stand
It reigns now, a mighty king

I created a monster
I gave it a mighty big name
It had no meaning whatsoever
Until I made it take the blame

9

What's the color of your tears?
Hopeless amber where all is lost
Blinding downpour of guilty fears
Painful lavender pays the total cost

Saturday afternoon – Stone Mountain freeway

*E*very *light in the world has been against me today. I don't want to be late, but it looks like I will.* Eric Henderson was driving the rental car he picked up at the Atlanta airport. He had just enough time to swing by the hotel and change before he hopped back into the car to make the drive to Stone Mountain from College Park. He had programed the GPS with the address, and he hoped the directions were correct for once.

He was so grateful to Royce for tracking him down. Just imagine, his son was getting married and he had graduated college with a good job. But Eric hadn't seen Jackie or her family in almost thirteen years. He was so anxious and a little bit scared. He really didn't know what Jackie's reaction to him might be. They had broken up with some pretty ugly words tossed back and forth between them.

Even though he had been back to Atlanta from time to time and year to year, Eric felt their relationship was never properly resolved. In fact, he hadn't seen the kids since Royce was about eight.

He had only wanted what was best for Jackie, but he guessed he'd gotten caught up in everything. There was no way his marriage to Lisa was going to last. From the first time he made love to Jackie, he knew she was the one. In fact, he knew he was in it for the long term. Everything would have turned out so differently if only he could have gotten her to see that.

Twenty-four years ago

When Jackie had told him she was pregnant, he had been ecstatic. He believed his dreams and prayers had come true. He knew the doctors hadn't known what they were talking about. He and Jackie celebrated that night and made love to the music of Luther Vandross. He could still remember her holding him tightly and kissing him over and over. She cried in his arms, and he was so grateful for it he almost cried tears of joy also. They showered together, and Jackie was so radiant. They laughed and ate a delicious steak dinner. They talked about baby names for a boy or girl. He was more than happy; he was grateful. It was the perfect night.

Everything was fine for the first six months or so, but as Jackie showed more and more, he was even more miserable in his marriage to Lisa. He wanted to be the one who rubbed Jackie's back and held her in his arms. He wanted to be acknowledged as the father. Not that bastard Jimmy. The thought of Jimmy getting to do all those things made him angry.

And when Jackie delivered a beautiful baby girl, Eric knew he finally had a chance. He wanted the whole world to know Chrystal was his because Chrystal looked just like him. He told Jackie that when he brought her flowers in the hospital, but Jackie didn't want to hear any of it. She pleaded with him to stay quiet. She reminded him how she had done all this to save her marriage, not destroy it. She said she loved Jimmy and knew he loved her even more so now. She said she also loved Eric for what he had given her, but she wanted to stay with Jimmy.

Eric couldn't forget that day. Her words hurt him so badly. He was bitter and angry, not only at Jackie but also himself. He vowed to stay out of their lives. He swore he was through with being used. He had gone home and finally told Lisa he didn't think their marriage was savable and he wanted out. Lisa didn't care; he had known that for years now. She gladly agreed to a quickie divorce after they settled on hefty alimony payments.

But it was torture seeing Jackie every day at work after she came back from maternity leave. He tried to stay away, he really did, but he couldn't help himself. First, he said he just wanted to check on them to make sure everyone was okay, especially when Jimmy was out of town. He didn't want anything to happen to his girls. Jackie didn't stop him. In fact, she encouraged him. He would still take her to lunch at least once a week, but she wouldn't meet him at hotels anymore. She said she really wanted her marriage to work. He had to be content with seeing her at work and occasionally coming to the house when Jimmy was away.

There was only one time when he had misunderstood Jackie and thought Jimmy was out of town when he wasn't. When he got to the house, Jimmy opened the door and looked at him sort of funny. "Oh, hi. Eric, right? What's up? Jackie didn't say you were coming over."

Eric quickly recovered and said, "I was just in the neighborhood and thought I would drop by and see how Jackie and Chrystal were doing. You know, just checking on them. I know sometimes you're out of town, and I kind of stop by every now and then to keep an eye out."

"Oh, sure, come on in. Jackie's in the kitchen. I think Chrystal is just about ready to wake up from her nap. I'll go and check. Jackie, Eric's here to see us."

Jackie had been furious. "What are you doing here? You know what I told you." Before Eric could say a word, Jimmy was back with a nine-month-old, sleepy Chrystal in his arms.

"Hey, Jimmy, can I hold her? She sure is a little cutie. She looks just like her beautiful mom."

It was so awkward that silence reigned in the kitchen.

After that incident, Jackie was especially careful to make sure he didn't come to the house when Jimmy was there, which meant he saw them less and less. It seemed he was becoming less and less important to her.

After his divorce was final from Lisa, Eric tried to move on. He asked for a location change to one of the satellite offices, thinking if he wasn't right beside Jackie each day, it wouldn't hurt as much. He only came to the main location every couple of weeks. Eric even dated some of the customer service reps at work, not the ones who reported directly to him, but others. They teased him about Jackie, saying they were just substitutes for her. He hadn't realized people had noticed their relationship. But being with anyone else was just so unfulfilling. The time dragged by. He tried to forget, but he couldn't.

It had been a year since Chrystal was born when Jackie started coming to work looking sleepless and unhappy. When he came to the office, he knew something bad had to be going on in her life, and he prayed he would be the one she turned to again. He didn't ask her anything, until one Wednesday afternoon when he happened to be passing her office and saw Jackie with her head in her hands.

"What's going on, Jackie? You look a little upset. I thought everything was going good. Is something wrong with Chrystal?" Eric was upset just seeing the hurt in Jackie's eyes.

"Hi. No. Chrystal's fine. I'm just ….. I don't know. I'm just tired, I guess. Jimmy's out of town again, and I guess I'm just a little lonely. Don't worry about it. I'm okay."

"Well, you don't seem okay. In fact, you seem pretty unhappy. What can I do to help? You know you only have to ask me, and I'll give you anything I have." Eric came into the office and closed the door. Now was his chance. "Let me help you. You know you want to. I promise I'll make no demands. We'll only do what you're comfortable with, no more, no less."

"I don't know. I want another baby. Things were so great at first with Chrystal. Jimmy stayed home and helped with everything. But now he's back to the out-of-town work trips and too tired for me and all that stuff. I don't know if I should even be thinking these thoughts. It's crazy. I can't keep asking you to help me. I have about—"

"No, I want to help. I would have to be crazy to turn down being with you. You know how I feel about you and Chrystal. I would do anything to be back in your favor. Just let me in again. I've missed what we had so much. You know I love you, and yes, I know you love me too. Just not the way I want and need. But if this is the only way I get to be with you, I'm willing and ready."

Eric knew it was wrong, but Jackie was his drug. Now that he had a hit, he wanted more and more. He convinced her to spend weekends with him, although it didn't take much convincing. Jackie seemed eager to go away with him. They took Chrystal with them out of town. They loved going to the North Georgia Mountains. It was only a three-hour car trip. They rented a little cabin and had glorious weekends.

Did he wonder about her husband and what he was doing to her marriage? Not at all. He figured if the man was stupid enough to let this wonderful woman roam free, then it was his duty to take care of her. Besides, Chrystal was his child. You could see it when they all were together. So many times, as they walked the quaint little streets of the mountain town, curious locals would come up to them and tell them what a beautiful family they had. Eric was so proud, and Jackie would smile broadly.

When they returned to the cabin and put Chrystal to bed, they would make love in front of the fireplace. It was so special and wonderful, and of course, it had to come to an end.

And then, Jackie was pregnant again. She was so happy and any-thing that made Jackie happy made Eric even more so. This time she didn't withdraw from him. They spent time together every chance they could. Chrystal was older and could tell Jimmy things he didn't need to know, so Eric persuaded Jackie to let her mom or sister babysit so they could have some time alone.

His house became their home, and he was on top of the world. They would leave work early or some days or never go in and go to his house instead. He would have to be lying to say the sex wasn't fantastic. She was everything he needed and wanted. Jackie was even more sponta-neous and quickly aroused than before Chrystal was born. He knew he benefitted from it time and time again. Sexually, she gave him all of herself, and he returned the favor. Still, there remained one part of her that he could never touch. He was in deep, but Jackie always held some of her emotions back. He wanted it all and was determined to make her let go of Jimmy.

That was the best time of his life, and Jackie told him over and over how happy she was too. She let him have a big role in her pregnancy this time. It really did feel like he was her husband, and he spoiled her with his gourmet cooking and lavished every comfort he could find on her.

He sometimes asked Jackie how things were around her house. She was evasive and wouldn't talk about it much. Eric wanted to believe that, this time, he really stood a chance. He did everything in his power to convince Jackie to stay with him and belong to him only.

Jackie delivered a healthy baby boy in January. Eric wasn't in the delivery room, but he was nearby. They named the baby Royce. Royce had reddish hair and light brown eyes. Again, the baby looked just like him. Eric was around as much as Jackie would let him be. For him though, it was never enough.

Then Jimmy stepped back into the picture. All of a sudden, he had time for Jackie and the children. He had a son, and Jimmy was so proud. Eric called him all kinds of fools. *How could you not know that these children aren't yours?* For one thing, they looked nothing like Jimmy. Eric knew that wasn't the definitive test, but he knew who had been making love with Jackie, and there was no way Jimmy did it enough to produce anything. He wanted to tell Jimmy the truth. He wanted to scream it from the top of Peachtree Plaza. He wanted so badly for Jimmy to just disappear. How happy everyone would be if Jimmy were permanently gone.

These thoughts consumed Eric. Again, he vowed to stay out of their lives. He couldn't take being near but not being able to touch or even see. He spent more time trying to get Jackie to let him see the kids than he actually saw them. And spending time alone with her was totally out.

If someone had told him he'd be caught in the middle like this, he would have laughed in their face. There would have been no way that he, Eric Henderson, would have let a woman pussy whip him into this corner he had been pushed into. It was hurting his manhood, his pride. He didn't like being in the shadows, and he was going to do something about it.

About nine months after Royce was born, Eric tried again to convince Jackie that she should divorce Jimmy and be with him. Jackie wouldn't hear of it. She said she loved Jimmy and nothing would make her leave him. Eric became so angry that he just couldn't take it anymore. He came to the house whether he thought Jimmy was there or not. He actually hoped Jimmy would be there and he could have it out with him. He and Jackie argued more than anything, and Jackie wouldn't let him in. After that, he felt like the fool. Jackie had totally used him just to produce babies for Jimmy. He felt like a stud horse.

Eric gave up. He finally had enough. He wanted more than to be her sometime lover. He didn't have any self-esteem left, and staying around watching Jackie do her thing between him and Jimmy had turned his stomach.

He didn't tell Jackie about it, but he started looking for jobs in other cities. After four months, he was finally offered a position in Charlotte,

North Carolina. He sold his house and made one final stop by her house in Midtown to tell Jackie he was leaving.

"Jackie, I love you, but I can't be on the outside anymore. I'm giving you one more chance. Come with me to Charlotte. We can start over, and I promise I will cherish you and our children for as long as I live. I've given up everything and everybody else to be with you. Can't you do the same for me?"

"Please don't do this," Jackie said. "You're so special to me. I've never had someone who cares for me the way you have. You make me feel so wonderful. You—oh Eric! I can't. I just can't. Why are you trying to make me choose? Why can't we just keep on doing like we have?" Jackie cried long and hard.

Eric held her as she shuddered and shook, but he was firm as he told her one last time, "You say I'm so special to you, but apparently not special enough. I feel like I've been used from the beginning." He raised his voice slightly and said, "Is that it? I was just your big dick to get the job done, but when you get satisfied you run home to Jimmy? My name isn't good enough to go on the birth certificate. All I get is a 'Thank you, Eric, for your sperm.' I gave you everything that Jimmy couldn't, and you still say you love your husband and can't leave him. Well, I wish I knew what he's giving you that I haven't!" When he finished talking he was practically shouting, and Eric knew he had gone too far.

Jackie pulled out of his arms and turned her back. "What the hell are you talking about? I never used you. You said you wanted to help me. I believed you when you said that."

She turned around and looked Eric in the eyes. "You said no strings. If I had known you'd try to destroy my marriage, I would never have agreed to do the things I did with you. I've never asked you for a penny for my children. Not that you have that much after paying Lisa off, but I still never asked."

Gray tears filled Jackie's eyes. "You knew where you stood from the beginning. Don't stand there now and act like you didn't get anything out of this relationship. You knew it was about the sex. And I admit the sex was the best ever, but I am *not* going to leave my husband and everything I've worked hard for, just for a big dick! If I had known you would act like this, I would have never let you fuck me!" Jackie looked like she might cry again, but she held strong.

"Oh, I understand now. I didn't get the whole damn picture before, but now I see you're just that big of a gold-digging fucking ho!"

Jackie's head snapped back like Eric had slapped her.

Eric continued, even though he knew he had gone beyond the point of return. "It's as clear as can be now. Good enough to fuck to get you pregnant, but not enough money to keep you in foreign cars and gold jewelry. Not enough cash to buy big houses in Midtown and eat at high-priced restaurants every night. I don't have the bank to keep you like you want to be kept. You know what. I got to leave before I do something stupid. Before you hate me more than you so-call love me." Eric grabbed Jackie as she turned her back to him again.

Jackie spun around out of his grip. "Don't you dare touch me, you son of a bitch. How could you say those things to me? You said you loved me, and this is how you treat me? How can you disrespect me, the mother of your children, this way? I don't know how I could have missed seeing the real you. As long as I do what you say, then great, but the minute I want to keep what I have, then I'm the whore. I wasn't fucking by myself. If I remember right, you were married at the time too. If I'm a whore, then you're the one who made me one! So I guess that makes you the pimp!" Jackie moved away from Eric, and dark tears of disgust and sadness rained down her cheeks.

"Jackie, please … I don't, I didn't mean—" Eric moved closer to Jackie and reached for her hand.

Jackie snatched her hand away and hugged her arms around herself. "You men are all the same. I don't know if the dick is even worth the shit we women have to put up with. Go on, get out, and don't come back with your whiny ass. I think I've used you enough. Maybe if I need another lover, I can find one with a bigger dick, who knows how to do what I tell him and shut the fuck up otherwise."

"Jackie, please. I'm sorry. I didn't mean the shit I just said. You know that. I just can't stand not being with you and Chrystal and Royce. You know it makes me crazy. I only—"

"That's enough. Just go. Please just go. I don't want to hear anything else from you."

Eric hung his head in defeat. He knew he didn't stand a chance now. "Can I at least see the kids before I leave? I promise no more drama."

"They're upstairs asleep. You know the way. I'll be in the kitchen when you're ready to go. Please make it quick." Jackie turned her back as Eric went upstairs to see the kids.

Eric finally came back downstairs, looking grim and emotionally wrung out. "Jackie, I'll keep in touch. Who knows, maybe one day … I don't like it, in fact I absolutely hate it, but I understand you love your husband. I wish it wasn't so. I wish you cared more for me. I wish—"

"Goodbye, Eric."

~

It took Eric over a year before he contacted Jackie and let her know where he was and how he was doing. That first phone call had been the hardest one he ever had to make. It was little more than: "This is my address and new phone number. Let me hear from you from time to time." He figured she didn't hang up, so maybe some of the anger had died down. Being away had cooled his head greatly. He threw himself into his new job with the Charlotte gas utility and moved ahead faster than he thought he would.

The next time he called, almost six months later, he asked if he could come by the next time he was in Atlanta. Jackie didn't say no. She just said, "Let me know beforehand." It was a baby step, but it worked. When he did see Chrystal and Royce, they didn't even know who he was. It hurt so badly. Jackie told the kids Eric was an old friend she used to work with. He had wanted to punch somebody. It was a good thing Jimmy wasn't there.

That's how it went for a few years. He would send cards full of money for their birthdays and Christmas. He usually made a twice-yearly trip to Atlanta to see Jackie and the kids, and Jackie was always happy to see him. She even told the kids he was like a brother to her. Eric knew he couldn't keep it up, waiting and hoping something went wrong between Jackie and Jimmy so he could step in and be the hero. It never happened, and he grew tired of the uncle part he was playing with his own children.

When Royce was about seven or eight, Eric made one last trip to Atlanta. He couldn't keep playing this game. Besides, he finally had someone in his life who meant a lot to him. He had met a woman who was beautiful, kind, and sweet, who stood beside him and wasn't ashamed to say, "This is my man." He brought her to Atlanta to meet Jackie and the kids.

"Jackie, I want you to meet Michelle Stanley. She means so much to me. You're one of my closest friends, and I wanted you to meet the woman in my life." He knew it was wrong to introduce her out of the blue like this, but Jackie had left him no choice. And he did love Michelle. She just wasn't Jackie.

"Hi, Jackie. Eric has told me so much about you. I can't wait to meet Chrystal and Royce also. You know this is a beautiful home you have. I just love all the black artwork."

Jackie's smile had frozen on her face when Eric introduced Michelle. "Michelle, you're welcome in our home anytime, and thank you, but Jimmy did most of the decorating. You know Eric means so much to me. I feel like we're much more than just friends. He's like the brother I never had."

Eric watched Jackie as she said this. *Like a brother, uh. Well I guess I deserved that,* he thought. Eric and Jackie turned as Jimmy came down the stairs.

"Oh, here's my husband. Jimmy, meet Eric's lady, Michelle. Isn't she just beautiful? Why don't you show Michelle our collection of art? She's very interested."

Jimmy greeted Michelle warmly and started showing her around. He tossed a "How you doing?" to Eric.

"Eric can I see you in the kitchen for a minute? You don't mind do you, Michelle?"

"Oh no, not at all. Jimmy is giving me a great art lesson." Michelle and Jimmy continued their discussion of Charles Bibbs's paintings.

∽

They stood in the kitchen just looking at each other. It was as if neither of them wanted to be the first one to say anything. Royce came running into the kitchen to give Eric a big hug.

"Uncle Eric, Dad just told me you were here. See how much I've grown since you were here last. I'm almost as tall as Chrystal. Chrystal's not here. She's over Cousin Nikki's house. Is that your girlfriend with Dad? She sure is pretty. Isn't she, Mom? I can't wait to show you the plane I've been working on. Let me go get it." They both turned to watch Royce race back out, but still neither said a word.

After a moment, Eric rubbed his hands together and said, "Wow. He sure has grown, but he didn't let me get a word in. Well, Jackie, what did you need to see me for? He tried to smile as he looked at her but too much hurt had occurred between them for him to be truly happy.

"Michelle is a beautiful woman," Jackie said. "She looks at you with genuine love in her eyes. You deserve someone to look at you that way. Do you love her? Do you love her like you once said you loved me?" Jackie looked away. "Does she know about us?"

"Jackie that's not fair. I don't—"

Jackie didn't wait for Eric to finish. Instead she asked him another question. "Are you going to marry her?"

Eric looked at Jackie and gently said, "If you were to say to me that you're ready to be mine only, no matter what, you're finished with this sham marriage to Jimmy, you're ready to pack up all your things, Chrystal and Royce's things, and come with me to Charlotte, then I would go into that living room and beg Michelle to forgive me. I would tell her I'm so sorry, but I love Jackie and have to be with her and my children. I would do that for you, Jackie. I would do that for us." Eric expelled a big breath.

Jackie wrung her hands and looked around the kitchen with teary eyes. "I'm forty-two years old next month," Eric told Jackie. "We aren't teenagers going through our first crush. I can't and will not keep holding myself back for you to make up your mind. If you can do this for me, then come on. Let's go. If not, then I'm going to walk into that other room, take Michelle's hand, and walk out of your life forever."

Jackie hesitantly said, "I wish you and Michelle all the happiness in the world. You deserve someone who truly loves you for you, who can give all her heart to you, freely. You deserve better than me. I can't give you what you need. I think I'm too damaged. I'm too afraid of the unknown. I love you, but I guess I just don't love you enough." Jackie hung her head, sighed and clasped her hands together.

"All right," said Eric. "I see. One last hug, okay." They clung to each other. Eric felt like Jackie didn't want to let go, but she finally did and stepped back. He knew he wanted to hold on to her forever but it seemed she had made up her mind once and for all.

She hung her head and breathed in deeply and then out. She took her hands and rubbed at her eyes, her face. She looked like she was counting how many breaths she took. Eric walked away.

∽ 10 ∾

What's the color of your tears?
Engorged yellow tides like the Yangtze swells
I'll ask once again and then no more
What's the color of your fears?

Saturday afternoon – at the reception

Old-school music blared from the speakers. Royce and Jessica had a deejay who was really spinning the tunes. Once the folks got their bellies full and their drink on, there was no stopping the fun. They made a Soul Train line, and everyone from Ms. Sylvi to Jade showed off their best dance moves. Laughter overflowed at the Faithful Dove. Jessica and Royce danced to a slow number from the Isley Brothers. Natalie and Earl were also on the floor. Everyone stood back and watched the beautiful couples. Wedding cake was being eaten and champagne and sparkling cider flowed. It was a wonderful time for everyone except Jackie.

She was still reclining where she had lain for more than twenty minutes. Tony held her hand and tried to get her to join the party. "Come on, Jackie, just one little bite. I know you'll feel better after you try this prime rib. It's juicy and delicious and so tender. Then we can join the party. Everyone's asking about you. You don't want to let them down, do you?"

"I just need a minute more, Tony. If I eat that beef, you'll be wearing it. I can't keep anything down. I just feel so terrible. Besides, it's not my wedding. No one's really missing me."

Jackie wasn't so much physically sick as emotionally exhausted. Her feelings had run the gamut from exhilaration to devastation in as little as an hour. Today had definitely not gone as she'd pictured and certainly not as she'd planned. In fact, the whole week had been one of the worst in her life. And she had plenty of miserable ones to compare it to. Jackie felt betrayed and belittled. She wasn't even important enough in her family's lives for them to tell her the truth.

It didn't surprise her that Chrystal had been seeing Jimmy. Chrystal was always a daddy's girl. Jimmy had meant a lot to Chrystal, and he could do no wrong in her eyes. But why hadn't she said so? It would have been so easy to just say, "Mom, I want to maintain a relationship with Daddy and keep him in my children's lives. You don't have to see him, but I want to." Jackie would have understood that. She wouldn't have liked it one bit, but she would have understood.

Now Royce, she didn't understand at all. Royce had never shown any interest in Jimmy. Jackie had no clue that Royce wanted to reunite with the man he considered his father. Obviously, Royce was the mastermind behind it all. She just didn't see Chrystal as smart enough to get them all back together. Jackie had believed her children had no knowledge of Jimmy's whereabouts, just as she hadn't. After today, she saw just how little knowledge she had of what her children were capable of. Somewhere along the way, the whole story must have come out about his relationship with Bryan. No one seemed surprised at all that Bryan and Jimmy were together. It seemed as if everyone was so accepting of their relationship.

And Royce had used her writing like he did. She had no memory whatsoever of him asking her to write his vows for the wedding. Was she that old and demented that she couldn't remember something as important as that? Was she intentionally blocking out what she didn't want to know?

Nancy barged right in and grabbed Jackie by the arm. "Come on, Jackie, enough of this fainting old lady thing. Get up, and come on out here and join the party."

"That's exactly what I told her, Nancy. I tried to get her to eat something first, but she's one stubborn lady." Tony stood back and let Nancy pull Jackie up.

"Okay, okay. Let me put my shoes back on. You know these are sitting-down shoes, not standing ups. But I'll do my best to be the proud mama and go out there and shake a tail feather." Both Nancy and Tony laughed at Jackie's antics, and they looked at each other with hope that she'd gotten over whatever had depressed her earlier.

Jackie came out of the lounge and had to smile in spite of herself. Everyone was having a wonderful time. Jimmy and Royce stood together sipping champagne and having a very amiable-looking conversation. They looked like they had never been estranged. Jessica, Bryan, and Natalie sat at the table having a chat. Bryan was flailing his hands about. It sounded as if they were discussing the decorations because she heard the phrase "dried rosebuds" much too often. All the guests were mingling and having a great time. Even Chrystal was chatting with one of Royce's groomsmen. He was kind of cute. Chrystal could do so much better than that Calvin person Nikki was clinging to. The grandmothers had most of the children huddled around them and were eating cake and laughing at the children trying to dance.

As she was deciding which group to join, Jackie saw the usher who had stopped them when they first arrived heading in her direction. *I wonder what this man wants now*, she thought.

"Mrs. Mattock," the usher said, "there's a last minute guest asking for you. He wants to join the festivities. Should I send him in?"

Jackie wondered who in the world would be arriving this late. *It was probably just one of her silly coworkers who got lost,* she thought. She didn't see her friend Barbara, so maybe that was who it was. "Yes, please show them in. It's never too late to celebrate." She was so preoccupied with her feelings that she really didn't pay attention to what the usher was saying.

Jackie had finally made her way around to Royce and Jimmy to bust up their little chat when she felt a light tap on her shoulder. Before she could turn around, she saw Royce's face spread in a big grin. "Mom, here's my surprise for you. I hope he makes you very happy."

Jackie spun around and looked into a pair of hazel eyes that she still saw in her dreams. "Eric, what are you … " This time her knees buckled, and she really did faint.

～☽

"Okay, everybody. Stand back and give her some air. Jackie, can you hear me? Are you all right?" A very worried Tony held Jackie's hand as Nancy placed a cool cloth on her forehead. Royce and Jessica hovered around the outside of the folks surrounding Jackie.

"Yes, I'm all right. What happened? Did I slip and fall? I have a terrible headache." Jackie tried to sit up, but Tony pushed her back down on the chaise. "Oh, Tony, I'm all right. Let me sit up. I think I just got too overheated, that's all. I just thought I saw somebody I used to know and—"

"Hi, Jackie. I was worried about you for a minute. If I had known my presence was going to make you black out, I might have stayed away." Eric leaned over Jackie and gave her a small smile. He took both her hands in his and asked, "How do you feel now?"

Jackie could only stare at Eric. She hadn't seen or heard from him in way too many years. But there he stood in the flesh. He looked just as good as the last time she saw him.

But the last time they parted had left her so distraught. She had been an emotional wreck for months. So many times, she wanted to call him and beg him to forgive her. To please come and take her away from this hell. Several times, she had the phone in her hand, ready to punch in the last number, but she always stopped. She couldn't do it to them. Michelle and Eric belonged together. She'd had her chance and she'd been too stupid to take it.

It was over ten years ago that Eric had begged her to come away with him. She remembered that last terrible day as if it was yesterday. Like a fool she had made him leave and afterwards she had gone upstairs to her bedroom. She pulled Jimmy to the side and told him that she suddenly felt sick. She didn't even come down when she heard Eric and Michelle leaving. She knew that if she stayed in the room with them, she would lose her mind. She wanted to touch Eric and knock Michelle's head off. She was so jealous, so hurt, so humiliated. Jimmy looked at her like she was a woman he didn't know. He was right. She didn't even know herself, but she did know that, after today, she would never be the same again.

She heard Royce beg Eric to make sure he came back soon. She lay on her bed, dry-eyed. There were no tears left. Her eyes felt like someone had been scratching at them with sandpaper. When Royce came to tell her Uncle Eric was gone, she still didn't get up. She just said, "I know baby." She lay there still when Chrystal came home and complained she didn't get to see Uncle Eric at all.

She still didn't come down, even when Jimmy called her for dinner. And when he finally came upstairs to check on her, she had nothing left to say. She didn't care what Jimmy thought about her actions. It didn't matter anymore what anyone thought. She knew she had risked it all and lost. To have this, she had to give up that. Somehow or other, this just wasn't worth it.

I want a chance again
To right the wrongs
The pain in your eyes
I want to erase it

I want a chance again
To do over
The things I didn't do right
The people I envied

I want a chance again
To laugh
Like I really mean it
Not afraid you will hear the lie

I want a chance again
To love you
With a true and honest passion
Not keeping you at arm's length

I want a chance again
To let the tears fall gently
Not ashamed to let you know
I am so very weak

After her divorce from Jimmy, Jackie wanted to call Eric even more and admit she had been so wrong, so blind to not have seen what was right there in her face. But her pride, such as it was, wouldn't let her. Jimmy had done a job on her. She didn't even feel worthy of love. How blind could she be, not to have seen Jimmy for what he was? She had prayed that Eric was out there somewhere happy, he and Michelle both.

Now, here he stood. Big, and bold, and oh so good-looking, right in front of her eyes. Her heart flip-flopped. "I don't understand. Why are you here?"

"Okay, everybody, let's give her some room." Nancy tried to steer all the onlookers back into the party room. "Everything's fine. Let's all go back to celebrating with the happy couple." Most folks hadn't seen what happened, but word had spread quickly and the music had come to a screeching halt. Rumors were flying about; some even said the groom's mother was dead. That rumor was started by Nikki.

Fortunately, it didn't take long to clear the small space. Everyone went about their business, except Royce, Jessica, Chrystal, Tony, Eric, and Jimmy.

"Mom, I invited Eric," said Royce. "When Jessica and I were making the guest list, we tried to think of all the people who were special to us. Of course, our immediate family came first, but I remembered how close you were to Eric when Chrystal and I were kids. I remembered how happy you always were when he came to town. I knew he was someone close to you. I wanted a way to thank you for all you've done for me, so I thought someone special from your past would lift your spirits."

"Oh, Royce, you didn't have to," said a bewildered Jackie with tears in her eyes.

Eric interrupted and said, "Yes, he did have to. I wouldn't have missed this day for anything. Unfortunately, I did miss the ceremony. I would have never forgiven myself if I'd missed out on the most special day for Royce and Jessica. I know it has been some years, too many years, but I never wanted to miss so much. I ask your forgiveness, and Royce and Chrystal, you too. I should have played a bigger part in all your lives. I never should have left the way I did."

Everyone looked at Eric with questions written all over their faces. Chrystal looked back and forth between Eric and Jimmy. "What's he talking about, Mom? I kind of remember Uncle Eric, but I always thought he was your friend back in the day. Why does it sound like he was so much more?"

"Yes, Jackie, why does it sound like he was so much more?" Jimmy purposely looked at Eric as he asked Jackie that question. "Eric, why don't you tell us all why you think you're so special to Jackie?" Jimmy took a step back and stood near the door as Bryan came into the room.

Royce spoke up first. "Dad, don't do this. Eric, you don't have to answer that. I wanted this as a special surprise for Mom. You guys are trying to turn it into something else. Jessica and I wanted to do something for Mom to show her she's loved and appreciated. Don't turn it into something sordid. Come on, Jessica. Let's get back to our wedding guests and let them have some privacy." Royce took Jessica's hand and tucked it under his arm as he led her back to the reception hall.

Jessica turned back as they neared the door and said, "We love you, Mama Jackie. Don't forget that Royce honestly loves you. No matter what anyone says or what else may happen."

Jackie didn't know what to say or do. Everyone was looking at her. She didn't have the answers to give them. She wanted to get up and run out like the coward she was. If it wasn't for those damn stiletto heels, she might have given it a try.

Jimmy and Bryan looked at her with smirks on their faces. She knew she didn't have to be a mind reader to tell what evil thoughts were going through their little hateful minds. Chrystal had aligned herself with Jimmy and Bryan. Jackie could tell by the confused look on her daughter's face that it didn't matter what she had to say. Chrystal wasn't going to believe her.

"I didn't mean to come here and cause trouble," said Eric. "I only wanted to be included in your lives, like I once was. But I think, if nothing else, Royce and Chrystal deserve some answers."

Before Jackie could say anything, Nancy came back into the room. "Jackie, Mom is worried sick about you. I think she's having some sort of panic attack. If you feel well enough, I think we should take her home and get you home also."

Jimmy said, "Okay, everybody. Let's get Ms. Sylvi home. I think we've had enough excitement here at the Peaceful Bird to last quite a while."

"Jim, honey, it's Faithful Dove," said Bryan as he patted Jimmy's arm and turned to go. "But I agree. Let's get Ms. Sylvi and Jackie home. We don't need any more drama than necessary."

Jackie wondered who the hell died and left these two misfits in charge. "I can speak for myself. Excuse you, Jimmy, and you, Mr. Bryan. I'm ready to get my mother and take her to a quieter location, but I don't want it to interfere with Royce and Jessica's festivities. Please don't make a scene. Nancy, please reassure Mama, and I'll meet you both at the van. Jimmy, if you want to do something, then let Royce and Jessica know we're heading back to my mother's house."

All this time, Tony hadn't spoken one word. Jackie could only wonder what he thought of all this. In fact, what did he think of her? Talk about dysfunctional. This was enough to make *The Jerry Springer Show*. She only hoped God was looking out for her, and after today, somebody would still love her.

"Jackie, let me help you to the van," said a totally confused-looking Tony. "In fact, I can take you on home if you want to skip the van ride. I know it's been a pretty rough afternoon." Tony helped Jackie stand and held an arm possessively around her waist. Eric watched them with a look of confusion and embarrassment.

"Thanks, Tony, but I'm going to gather any dignity I have left and go see about my mother. You've been too sweet already." Jackie hugged Tony back and patted him on his shoulder as she gave him a small kiss on the cheek. "I didn't mean to worry anyone. It seems I've upstaged the happy couple. Will you please give my apologies to Jessica's family? I don't want to cause any more disruptions."

"All right. I'll give you a call later tonight, just to check on you, okay?" Tony kissed Jackie on her forehead and looked questionably at Eric as he exited the room.

Jackie saw that Eric was still silently, waiting in the room along with Chrystal. She couldn't look him in the eyes. She felt so guilty. "Chrystal, please see if there's a side door I can go out of to get back to the parking lot. I really don't want to have to go through the entire reception area."

"Mama, exactly what's going on here? I never noticed before just how much Royce and Uncle Eric look alike. I guess I wouldn't have noticed now if they didn't happen to be standing together like that. Just please tell me the truth."

Jackie stared blankly at her dress and started picking at a piece of imaginary lint. Chrystal looked at Jackie with tears in her eyes. She turned to Eric and asked him, "Uncle Eric, why does Royce look so much like you? In fact, I probably look a lot like you too. What did you mean when you said we deserved to know the truth?"

"Let's get your mom and grandmother home," Eric said. "Then we can all sit down and talk. Do as your mother asked and see if there's a side door. I'll bring her around to it just as soon as you let us know."

"Okay. I'll be right back." Chrystal hurried from the room, but as she was about to close the door behind her, she said, "And I want all the truth. Not just the pretty parts."

Jackie stood and hugged her arms around herself as if she was cold. *She's a beautiful woman with strength and determination etched in her features,* thought Eric. He probably loved her more than ever. But would the scared look ever leave her eyes?

"Why did you come back? Why didn't you just stay away?" Jackie asked. "I'd gotten you out of my system years ago, and here you pop up again. I can't, I won't go through this anymore."

"You don't have to go through this anymore." Eric moved even closer to Jackie, looking directly in her eyes.

"You can't keep your promises, can you?" Jackie asked. "You said you would walk out of my life forever that day. So where's Michelle?" Her voice broke on the last word, and she hugged herself even tighter. She looked to the ceiling, the floor, anywhere, as if the answers were written somewhere in the room, but she wouldn't look at Eric.

Eric took her hands away from rubbing her arms and held them within his own. "You know I can't. You know me better than anyone, and I've never been able to stay away from you. I don't know why, and I really don't even care why anymore. I just know my life has never been the same since that day in your office when I dried your tears with a kiss."

"You always knew just what to say to me, to calm me, to get me to do what you wanted." Jackie pulled her cold hands out of Eric's warm ones and gave a sad little laugh with a shake of her head.

"No, I just enabled you to do what you really wanted to. I made it easy for you to let go and accept. That's all. You didn't do anything you didn't want to. You may have told yourself that, but you and I both know the truth."

Jackie shook her head no. Even now, Eric saw, she still wanted to deny the truth. She wiped at her eyes with her other hand and shuddered as if she were cold.

Eric slowly raised his hand to touch Jackie's face, but she moved back out of reach. He wondered if it really was too late for them. "I don't even know what to call what we have. I've had every damn emotion in the dictionary, and that's hard for a man like me to admit. I'm not a little boy anymore. I know what I want. You're not a little girl either. Do you know what you want?"

Jackie vehemently shook her head at Eric. "I just want to be happy. I want someone to love me for me, not for any purpose, not for any grand plan. That's all I ever wanted. And if you can't do that, then just leave me alone."

"Well, it looks like you might have gotten your wish, for love that is. Who's the young man who wants to play knight in shining armor to your damsel in distress? He looks like a lost puppy happily following behind his next mistress."

Anger flared in Jackie's eyes. "Just what are you trying to say? I don't have that kind of power over anyone, and I don't know what you mean by 'damsel in distress.' I don't need a puppy, boy, or man—not even you—to save me."

Jackie gave Eric a troubled look as she moved to sit back down on the chaise. "But you didn't answer me. Where's Michelle?" she asked with teary eyes but with steel in her voice. She wasn't playing games, and Eric could see it.

Eric sat down beside Jackie and again reached for her hand, but she clasped her hands together in her lap. "Michelle and I broke up soon after that last day at your house. When we got back to Charlotte, she said she'd noticed some pretty disturbing things."

"Disturbing things? What kind of things did she think she noticed?" Jackie asked in an accusatory voice.

"She said she couldn't compete with you. Not even from hundreds of miles away. She said she loved me, but she didn't think I was capable of loving anyone other than you. She said she couldn't stand in the way of true love."

Jackie looked at Eric and gave him a sad smile. "Oh, I see. We're both such a piece of work. We don't even know how to treat ourselves, so we definitely can't do right for others. I tried long and hard to forget you, and look where it's gotten me."

"You're a beautiful, mature woman with a sincere and kind heart. You need much more than a boy in your life. It's time to claim what you really want and stop playing this game."

"Stop! I don't want to hear any more. I know what I want. I just want to be left alone and in peace. What will it take to make you understand that?"

Eric kept right on talking as if Jackie hadn't said anything. "You know, I didn't argue with Michelle when she said those things. I didn't even try to convince her she was wrong. In fact, I couldn't say anything in my defense. Because I knew it was the truth. I let her walk out of my life so she could find someone who was worthy of her. So who has taken over your heart? Who's the guy that spoiled you for anyone else? Is it junior out there?"

"You can't be serious. You haven't heard a word I've said. Do you see me here with anyone else? I'm sad to say I haven't even dated much in all these years. And all this while I prayed you were happy somewhere and doing well, but every time I looked at Royce, all I saw was you. And I couldn't forget what we had, what we did. How about you? Did you ever try with anyone else? Anyone other than Michelle?"

Eric took Jackie's hands in his again. This time she let him. He rubbed his thumb over her cold knuckles. "Sure, I tried. I'm not going to lie. I needed female companionship. There have been several women after Michelle. None of them lasted long. None of them could make me forget you."

Eric stood and pulled Jackie up with him. He encircled her smaller frame with both of his arms and held her tightly. "I even moved from Charlotte to Chicago. I wanted to put more distance between you and me, and believe me, the winters there can make you forget a lot. But as hard as I tried to put us behind me, I just couldn't. I wasn't happy, and I felt so lonely. I thank the Lord that Royce found me." He smiled and then kissed the top of her head.

"I did everything I could not to show up on your doorstep and camp out until you let me stay." Eric gave a sad laugh full of longing and hopelessness. "So what do we do now? Here I am again. I keep popping up, as you say. So what are you going to do about it?"

"Okay, Mom, Eric. It seems I interrupted something. There's a side door back behind this hallway. I'm ready when you guys are. I already took the kids to the van, and we're all ready to go. I'm ready to hear what you have to say anytime now."

~⁓

Saturday evening – Ms. Sylvi's house

Jackie helped her mother out of the van. The ride to the house had been so quiet. Even the children didn't carry on. They all went to sleep as soon as the van hit the interstate. Eric had followed them in his car back to the house. Jackie didn't trust herself to ride with him. It seemed the time had finally come. She didn't feel very brave. In fact, she was terrified. After all these years, the chickens had finally come to roost.

"Let's get settled, and then we can all have a little talk," said a visibly tired Nancy. "Chrystal, let me help you get the babies to their room. I hope they stay asleep, at least for a little while. Jackie, here's Eric. Why don't you and Eric help Mom, and I'll be right back." Nancy was handling everything with her usual military efficiency. Jackie was thankful for it.

Jackie sat on the sofa across from her mother. Eric sat at the opposite end. She looked around the room she knew as well as she knew her own home. There were plenty of happy memories associated with this house. Ms. Sylvi and Buddy had matching chairs that sat side by side, and Jackie couldn't help but notice Buddy's empty seat. She didn't want to be nervous, but she couldn't stop wringing her hands together. She was a grown woman for God's sake. Finally, she looked at Eric, and he gave her a small smile.

Chrystal and Nancy came out of the back, and Chrystal stood next to the sofa across from her mother.

Nancy broke the ice. "Okay, the babies are still asleep, thank the Lord. Does anybody need anything, water, soft drink, narcotics, a judge?" she asked with a tired smile on her face as she leaned against the wall beside her mother.

No one said anything.

"Then let's have this little talk," said Nancy.

Ms. Sylvi looked out the front window. "Oh, here come Jimmy and Bryan. We might as well let them get seated before whoever needs to say something tells us whatever they need to," she said sadly.

Chrystal moved to open the door for her father. She kissed him on the cheek as he and Bryan came in.

Jimmy scanned the room in one long look. He seemed to be too pleased with himself. He and Bryan both had secretive smiles on their faces, and Jackie wondered what he was up to now.

"Royce and Jessica decided to leave on their honeymoon," Jimmy explained. "He said whatever went on here could wait until they got back, and we could inform him then. I agree with him, since I've been talking with him about the possibilities and outcome of this little talk." Jimmy moved over to the opposite sofa from Jackie, and he and Bryan took a seat.

Eric took a deep breath and looked at Jackie. "Royce called me several months ago. He said he was getting married. Believe me when I say I was surprised. I hadn't realized how many years had gone by. I had long since lost contact with Jackie, on purpose. Royce and I had a wonderful conversation, and we continued to talk over the next few months."

Bryan fidgeted in his seat and looked at Jimmy. They acted as if they were planning something by the look that passed back and forth between them.

"As you know, Chrystal," Eric said, "I used to come around when you guys were little. Royce remembered me and the close relationship we used to have."

Jimmy made a rude noise in his throat and everyone looked his way. "I'm sorry. I think I need a drink of water. Go on, Eric. Don't let me stop you from telling your tale," said Jimmy as he pretended to clear his throat.

"Well, I was a little hesitant. I didn't know, until Royce told me, that Jackie and Jimmy had been divorced for several years. Royce said he and his fiancée wanted me at their wedding. He explained that Jackie had been somewhat depressed and he wanted to cheer her up by surprising her with an old friend. I couldn't believe the detective work they'd put into tracking me down. I said yes. I wanted to come to the wedding for them and for my own selfish reasons. Also, I wanted to be there to be recognized as part of the family."

Jimmy made another noise and looked at Jackie slumped in the corner of the sofa. She had dingy tears streaming down her cheeks and wouldn't look up.

"I figured it was now or never. Too many years and too few words have gone by. I love your mother, Chrystal. Not as an old coworker and certainly not as a brother. I've been in love with Jackie since before you were even born." Eric looked directly at Jimmy as he said this, daring Jimmy to say something now.

"Mom, what's he trying to say?" asked Chrystal. "Did you and Eric have an affair? Is that what's going on?"

Jackie started to say something, but Jimmy spoke up. "It's more than just that, Chrystal. It's possible that Eric is your and Royce's father," said Jimmy as he calmly leaned back on the sofa. "I say there's a possibility, but that doesn't necessarily mean he is. Your mother isn't the only one who can keep a secret."

Eric wanted to bust Jimmy in the mouth, but he knew violence wasn't the answer. Instead, he said, "Chrystal, it's more than just a possibility. It's a fact."

Chrystal looked at all the people involved. She looked even more confused than before they started. "I don't understand. Mama, what's Daddy talking about?"

Ms. Sylvi spoke up for the first time. "I don't think y'all need all of us for this conversation. Come on Nancy, and you too Bryan. Let's go into the kitchen and make some coffee." Nancy moved to help Ms. Sylvi up, but Jackie finally spoke.

"No, Mama. Stay there, Nancy and Bryan too. I don't want to have this conversation but once. I want everyone to hear it firsthand so we all know the same thing, so there won't be any miscommunication."

Jackie exhaled a shaky breath and plunged ahead. "Jimmy is right, I have been keeping secrets, but I'm not the only one. Jimmy and I got divorced because of Bryan and what they really are to each other. They've been in an affair since before Jimmy and I were even married. I was just too blind to see what was right in my face. I guess I didn't want to see it. I found out later that our marriage was just a front for Jimmy to look legitimate. It was something I never would have willingly been involved with if I had known."

Ms. Sylvi gasped and started fanning herself with her hand. Nancy put an arm around her and patted her shoulder. Nancy gave Jimmy a dirty look, like she wished she could slap that stupid smile off his face. Bryan looked at Eric, and Eric gave him one of those "yeah, you too, bitch" looks.

Jackie continued in a shaky voice. "I wasn't happy in my marriage, and I went looking for someone to love me. I tried to convince myself that I was unhappy because I couldn't get pregnant. I knew something was wrong from the beginning, but I didn't want to believe someone I thought I loved would be that cold-blooded and evil. But Eric was there for me."

Jackie turned to Eric and said, "He was everything good that Jimmy wasn't. He was more man in his little toe than Jimmy had in his whole body."

Bryan now made a rude noise and started to protest, but Eric held up his hand to silence him. Jackie looked at Jimmy and went on with her confession. "He made me feel special. He loved me and I used him for my own selfish reasons, and I am so sorry. I used him and continued to lie to myself and to him."

Jackie took another big breath and continued. "I stayed in a loveless sham of a marriage out of pride, greed, stupidity, and any number of other reasons that had nothing to do with what was right. I could say I was young and got caught up. I could say a lot of things, but the truth is I made the biggest mistake of my life when I married Jimmy. Jimmy never wanted me as a true wife. He was already in love with Bryan. I realized way too late that I wanted Eric. I loved Eric."

Jackie looked at a wide-eye Chrystal and said, "Yes, Eric is your and Royce's father."

Jimmy gave a sinister chuckle and said, "Well, you're half right, Jackie. Eric is Royce's biological father, but Chrystal is mine." Jimmy stood up and looked directly at Jackie and gave her a sly grin.

Both Eric and Jackie said, "What?" at the same time.

"You didn't really think I was that blind or stupid, did you?" asked Jimmy. "I knew everything wasn't as platonic between the two of you as you wanted me to believe."

Jackie looked at Jimmy and just shook her head. "How long have you known? Why didn't you say something?"

"I've known the paternity since right before Oro was born. I'd suspected you were unfaithful since Chrystal was born. After you called me about Chrystal's predicament, I got in contact with her. She came to visit me after Jewel was born, and I had a paternity test done on her, among other things. The next time she came to visit, she had Royce with her. I had a test done on him also. How you could have let a sixteen-year-old get into that kind of trouble, I'll never know."

Jimmy continued to smirk at Eric. "And yes, Jackie, unlike you, I told them the reason we got divorced. Bryan was there, and I wanted to get everything out in the open for once. We felt Chrystal and Royce were old enough to understand."

Jackie looked at Chrystal with sadness in her eyes. "Chrystal, I can't believe you never told me. How could you have gone on letting me believe you didn't have anything to do with your father? Why? And Royce knew too?"

Jimmy nodded his head yes.

"I guess you all were having a great big laugh behind my back. 'Look at stupid Jackie. She still doesn't have a clue.' All this time, and you all knew. You let me be eaten up with shame and remorse, trying to protect you both."

Chrystal hung her head and muttered, "Mama, I was so angry with you for the longest. I knew it wasn't all your fault, but I guess, I wanted to blame you for making Daddy go away. I wanted us to be a big happy family, and I thought you messed that up for all of us." More loudly, Chrystal said, "I guess I figured that was a way to get back at you. I knew something you didn't, but not about the paternity tests. I swear I never knew anything about that. But I knew where Daddy was and that he loved me and he loved the kids too." Chrystal sniffed and wiped at her cheeks with the back of her hand like a little girl.

"Wait a minute. Let me get this straight." His anger growing, Eric stood in front of Jimmy. "You had a paternity test done on Chrystal and Royce, and only Royce is my child?"

Jimmy glared at Eric and just as angrily said, "I guess that comes as a shock to you, big guy, since you and Jackie were probably screwing your whoring asses off behind my back every chance you could get!"

"Jimmy, don't you dare talk about Jackie like that. She's my daughter, and she may not have done the wisest things, but you apparently went into the marriage being even more dishonest and sinful." Ms. Sylvi leaned back into her chair as if all the life had been drained out of her. "Nancy, help me to my room. I don't think I need to hear any more. I understand enough. I love you, Jackie, no matter what, and even you, Jimmy, but I just can't overlook how you and Bryan, you know, live."

Jimmy looked at Bryan and hung his head. He was not ashamed of his and Bryan's relationship but Ms. Sylvi's comments did make him pause. He wanted Ms. Sylvi on his side and now he wasn't so sure she would be.

Nancy moved to help Ms. Sylvi to her bedroom.

Jackie looked up with tangerine tears streaming down her face. "Mama, I'm so sorry you had to find out this way. I never meant to disrespect you."

Ms. Sylvi nodded her head but couldn't say any more.

Jackie lowered her head. More than anything else, she was most ashamed that her mother had to hear about her like this. And as much as she hated Jimmy, she didn't want the relationship between her mother and him to be destroyed. She pulled herself together and asked Jimmy another question. "So if you knew all this, all this while, why didn't you just say so? Why all the secrets, Jimmy?"

Jimmy looked at Jackie and Eric with fire in his eyes. "Frankly, I didn't think you deserved to know. You've done me no favors over the years. Besides, you apparently were trying to pass off somebody else's child as mine. If you weren't sure then, who was I tell you differently?"

Jackie stared back at her ex-husband. "Jimmy, you're one of the most despicable people I've ever had the misfortune of dealing with. How could I have ever thought I loved you?" Jackie flung her hand in Bryan's direction and said, "You and this thing here deserve each other. You're just Thing One and Thing Two!"

"What's that supposed to mean, Jackie? Just who are you trying to talk about?" Bryan said as he tried to jump in the middle of the conversation.

Jackie totally ignored Bryan and asked Jimmy, "Does Royce know Eric is his biological father?"

"He does now. I knew I wasn't the father, therefore Eric had to be, unless you were that big of a whoring slut and was with somebody besides him."

Nancy came back into room at just that moment. "I don't know all that was just said, and it really doesn't matter, but from what I just heard, I have to agree with Mama. You, Jimmy, are the last one fit to call Jackie names. She's my sister, and I love her. She did what her heart told her to. You, on the other hand, have to be the biggest, nastiest piece of shit I have ever seen. You and Bryan both deserve each other."

"Wait a minute, missy," said a flustered Bryan. "Don't you dare talk about my man like that. He has been the best thing to ever happen in my life. I will not sit here and let you talk about—"

"All right, everybody. I think we've gotten off subject," said Eric. "We've all done our share of wrong. There's no need to call anyone names, especially you Jimmy. We all need to respect all the people in this room. We're all related some sort of way, and we need to remember that. Now calm your ass down, Bryan. Nobody invited you here anyway."

Bryan huffed and sat back down, muttering to himself. Jimmy patted him on the knee and said, "Don't worry. It's going to be all right."

Eric had enough. "Jackie, can I see you in the kitchen for a minute?" He wanted to gather Jackie up and take her home. Given the chance, that was exactly what he was going to do.

"Eric, I really didn't want things to come down to this. My mother is ashamed of me and probably thinks I'm the biggest slut around. My daughter hates me, and my sister is exhausted but still trying to defend me. I don't know what Royce thinks, like I ever knew. And you, you shouldn't have to put up with the evil that Jimmy and Bryan throw around. I wish I'd never met Jimmy."

"Don't say that. If that was the case, you and I wouldn't be standing here in your mother's kitchen today. I truly believe there's a reason for everything. If things hadn't gone on before as they did, then where would we be now?"

Eric drew Jackie to him and hugged her tight. They could still hear arguing going on in the living room.

"I've never made a secret of my feelings for you, Jackie. Nothing has changed for me."

Jackie hugged Eric back and silently inhaled his scent. It brought back so many memories.

"But that Jimmy is something else. I kind of always thought he was gay. Otherwise, the way he treated you just didn't make sense. And that little Bryan guy, now he takes the cake with a lot of frosting on top. He's too sweet."

They both chuckled.

"I was surprised, though, when Jimmy said he had done the paternity tests and only Chrystal was his, but that hasn't changed my feelings for you all one bit." Eric held on to Jackie more tightly.

"You know I hate to confess this but I feel like I have always known that Chrystal was Jimmy's biological daughter. It was just a feeling you know. I wonder if that is why I always looked at Chrystal differently. I wanted you to be the father so badly but deep down inside I knew the truth." Jackie struggled to blink back tears. She buried her face in Eric's chest.

In a muffled voice she said, "I think I have done Chrystal an injustice all her life. I think I blamed her for Jimmy's behavior. Oh Eric, I really believe, on some innate level that I made Chrystal the whipping boy for Jimmy and my problems. I feel so ashamed that I wasn't a better mother to her."

Jackie was visibly shaken and struggled to accept a truth that now made so many things much clearer.

Eric rubbed Jackie's back and wiped away her tears. "You have done everything in your power to make a good life for Chrystal and for Royce. You have nothing to be ashamed for. I have seen the love you showered on both of your children and I don't want to hear you blame yourself for Jimmy's wrongdoings."

Jackie tried to believe Eric's words but deep down inside she blamed herself for the strained relationship between her and Chrystal. She exhaled a shaky breath and hugged Eric tighter.

"I do have something I need to tell you though. If everything's coming out, then I need to come clean too."

Jackie pulled back out of Eric's arms and looked into his eyes. "Please don't tell me any more secrets. I don't think I can take it. All that matters is that you're here now and that the truth has finally come out."

Jackie moved to the refrigerator and rummaged around. She took out a can of soda and offered Eric one as she slowly opened the top. "I can't believe that damn Jimmy. All these years, and he kept quiet. And Chrystal too. Well, I can believe that of her considering how I treated her, but not Royce. Not my baby. How could he have done that to me?"

Eric shook his head no to the soda but said, "I don't know, Jackie. I wish I could say Royce did it to protect you, but I just don't know Royce that well. Just another bad mistake on my part because I thought both of your children were mine, but even then, I still didn't do what I should have as their father."

Eric took Jackie over to the table and sat down. "I know I have to tell you the truth though, or my conscience will never let me sleep. I want whatever kind of relationship we have from this day forward to be one based on truth and honesty."

"All right, well, is this a drink-of-soda telling, or do I need to bring out the big guns and get Mama's bottle of whiskey?" Jackie smiled a real smile as she saw Eric's eyes light up with joy.

"Well, let me just say it, and then we'll see. I might need that whiskey no matter what. Okay. Remember when you came to me about getting pregnant? Well, I never told you all of the truth. I made it sound like Lisa didn't want children, but there was more to it than that."

Jackie gave Eric a questioning look, but she continued to sip at her soda. "We'd tried to have children, but with no success. She and I both went to the doctor, and the problem was with me. The doctors said I had a low sperm count. They said I'd probably never be a father."

"Are you telling me you went into this knowing you couldn't get me pregnant? How could you have lied to me about something like that? I told you how important it was to me and you—why Eric?" Jackie picked at the placemats on the table. She felt betrayed all over again.

"Listen, Jackie, please. The doctors didn't say it was a definite no. They said in all likelihood I couldn't have children, but you see, God had a plan, no matter what the doctors said. I know it was wrong, but I wanted you so much. I loved you even then. Jackie, please look at me."

"Go on. I'm listening. I don't think I want to look at you just now. I want to understand what you're saying. I've listened for too long, but I still don't seem to hear."

"I don't know how to say it any plainer. When you had Chrystal, I thought all my prayers had been answered and yours too. I knew how much you wanted a baby. I didn't say anything because here was the baby as living proof. And then when Royce was born, I knew I had been doubly blessed. Please, just give us a chance, a real chance."

"I don't know. I've had too many surprises today. I feel … I don't know how I feel. I just want to go home and go to sleep. I don't think I can take another anything right now."

"I understand. Please let me take you home then. I won't try to come in or anything. I just want to make sure you get home safely."

"Okay, I'll let you do that. But I need time. I know we're not getting any younger but today, today has been one hell of a day."

Nancy sat down beside Chrystal on the sofa. "Chrystal, how could you do your mother like this? I've seen her fight hard to do everything she could for you and Royce. How could you think she was the only problem behind your parent's breakup? The look on her face when crazy Jimmy told her like that, it was just so sad."

Jimmy and Bryan were huddled together over on the other sofa, deep in conversation.

"Aunt Nancy, you just don't understand. You weren't in the house with us. You don't know what it was like for me. Daddy loved me, but it seemed like Mama just didn't want us to be together. It was like she was jealous of the relationship we had. I don't know. I just don't know what I was thinking."

Chrystal stood up and walked over to the glass door and looked into the yard. "I thought if I had something to use, to bargain with. I thought maybe Mama would do what I wanted her to. I don't know. It's been so hard for me. She only had eyes for Royce. Royce could do no wrong. Everything was about Royce. Royce was the golden child. Nobody loved me but Daddy, and when he went away, I felt like nothing." Chrystal broke down and cried like a little girl. There was nothing rough or tough about her now.

Jimmy and Bryan stopped talking and watched Chrystal at the door. Bryan started to go to her, but Jimmy held him back. He got up and went to his daughter and hugged her tight. "Chrystal, your mother has loved you from day one. I guess I didn't help any by filling your head with my anger at her, but she has never done anything to hurt you or Royce. It was always about what was best for you."

'But, Daddy, I saw and heard how she treated you. I wanted to run away so many times. I hated being with her and Royce." Chrystal wiped at her eyes. They shone, golden with tears.

"Yes, I know that's how you felt. But it was partly how I made it look. It was what I wanted you to believe. I didn't think about much back then except what I wanted."

Bryan came over to the door and stood on the other side of Chrystal and hugged her. "This isn't easy for me to admit," Jimmy said, "but your mother put up with a lot. I didn't treat her right from the beginning. I wasn't true to myself." Jimmy looked at Bryan over Chrystal's head and smiled.

"I loved you all the best way that I could, but when things went bad, I only wanted to hurt your mother for leaving me like she did. You and Royce didn't know everything that went on, and there's no reason you should have. I've done some terrible things to your mother. You both were children and, I thought, easy to manipulate. And I tried to turn you against her. For that, I'm sorry. I never meant for things to get this way. Please forgive me."

"I want to, Daddy. I want to more than anything. I want to love Mom like a true daughter should, but I've made too many mistakes, done too many things I that I'm so ashamed of. I don't know if she can forgive me. I just wish I could forgive myself."

∽

Jackie and Eric slipped out of the house through the kitchen door while everyone was still in the living room talking. She called Nancy from her cell phone and told her she had left and Eric was taking her home.

"Jackie, just go and take care of your business, if you know what I mean, wink-wink." Nancy gave a deep chuckle that made Jackie smile. "Everything's going to be all right here. I think things have finally calmed down. I'll look after things and let Mama know. And, Jackie, don't worry. We love you."

Jackie had given Eric the address for her house, and he programmed it into the GPS. They were quiet as they traveled from Ms. Sylvi's house to Jackie's. Eric let the jazz station play on the car's XM system.

Jackie leaned her head back on the headrest and closed her eyes. She tried to sleep, but sleep seemed to be dodging her efforts left and right. She was replaying the day over in her mind, but she must have dozed off eventually because the next thing she heard was Eric opening her car door and calling her name.

"This is a really nice neighborhood," said Eric. "Even in the dark, I can see the well-manicured lawns, and your house is quite a beauty. I wouldn't have expected anything less." Eric helped Jackie out of the car and stood back as she rummaged through her Louboutin bag for the house key.

"Well, you might as well come on in. It would be ungrateful for me to just leave you standing out here, especially after everything that happened today." Jackie walked the short path to the front door. "I don't usually come through the front door. I drive my little baby into the garage and come through the kitchen. Well, anyway." She knew she was babbling, but she was suddenly very nervous. She had known Eric for over twenty years, but in some ways, they were strangers.

Jackie let them both into the foyer of her ranch home. She hurried over to the alarm system and turned it off. "Welcome to my little home. Let me turn on a few more lamps so we won't be stumbling in the dark."

The foyer opened into a great room with a fireplace. It was decorated in a style that could only be called Jackie-ism, a little shabby chic, a lot bohemian, mixed with mid-century modern. "Well, what do you think? I'll give you the grand tour, but first I have to kick off these killer shoes. My feet have been crying all day. I told Nancy these were sitting-down shoes. Definitely not standing, and walking is totally out."

Eric laughed along with Jackie and helped her balance as she slipped off her shoes, which made her several inches shorter and so her head was only up to his shoulders.

"I know what you mean," said Eric.

"I'm usually not a suit-and-tie guy myself as you know. I feel like this shirt has become a second skin. Do you mind if I take off the tie at least?"

"Do whatever makes you comfortable. You can take off your shoes too if you want."

Eric took off his jacket and loosened the tie and took it off. He rolled up his shirt sleeves, and kicked off his loafers, and finally breathed a sigh of relief. Jackie stared at him. There was only a little lighter brown hair mixed in with the reddish brown. He was still in great shape too. The years had been very kind to him. She had to stop herself from reaching out and touching his arm.

"Okay. The kitchen is this way." She said a little breathlessly. "I didn't need a formal dining room. I just have the eat-in space with the keeping room." There she went again, running off at the mouth. She really was nervous.

"Whoa! It looks like someone has broken in and made a disaster of your beautiful kitchen." Eric looked around the kitchen and saw mess all over the floor. There was dried something on the stovetop and peas and carrots on the café-style table and chairs. Sticky syrup was dribbled all over everything. Empty glasses and plates were stacked on every surface. "There's a trail of gooey stuff going down this hallway. Does this lead to the bedrooms?"

Jackie was so embarrassed. She had forgotten about her little pity party of the night before. In their rush to leave earlier, she hadn't paid much attention to the state of her house. It was a total mess. She couldn't believe she had done that much destruction. She must have been totally out of her mind with liquor.

"The only person who broke in here and made this mess was me. I came home last night after the rehearsal dinner and had myself a little breakdown party with Mr. Gin and Mrs. Tequila. In fact, Nancy found me this morning with my head in the toilet. I didn't realize just how far gone I was."

Eric reached out to Jackie's face and gently touched her cheek.

"I don't even want to look at my bedroom and bathroom," Jackie said. "I do remember some of the craziness that went on in there." She turned her back to Eric and ran her fingers through her curly hair. "I guess I need to clean this up before it really starts to smell."

"Come on and show me where the cleaning supplies are, and I'll help you. Can I ask what got you so upset?"

Jackie went over to the pantry and pulled out a broom and some extra paper towels. She went to the sink and brought out the cleanser and some sponges from underneath. "There are some dishtowels in that drawer beside the stove and plenty of hot water. There's also a mop and bucket in the laundry room right there with some Pine-Sol. It looks like we're going to need it all."

"Jackie, what made you want to get drunk and do this?" Eric spread his hands out indicating the kitchen. "What happened?'

Jackie sighed and said, "I guess I finally started feeling my age. You know I'm no spring blossom. I'll be fifty this November." Keeping her back to Eric, Jackie filled the sink with water.

"I know. I remember your birthday. It's the twenty-second." Eric started sweeping up food. "But that shouldn't have made you this despondent. This looks like you were trying to forget something. Was it me?"

"Maybe. I came home last night and it was so quiet, and I guess I realized that was how it was going to be from now on. I felt lonely and lost. I felt like nothing. Then I started thinking back to how it started with us." Jackie loaded the dishwasher with all the dirty dishes and cleaned the stovetop and counters. "I questioned all of it, and I came up lacking. Not from the love we shared, but the emotional roller coaster I let control me, which unfortunately got out of hand. I thought I knew me, but I was wrong. I'd somehow become a bitter old woman." She stood with her back to the dishwasher and watched Eric get the mop and bucket ready.

"Do you regret it? Do you wish you never met me?" Eric started mopping the floor.

"No, I don't think I regret it. I wish I had done things differently. But like you said earlier, if we'd never met, then everything that's good wouldn't be. I wouldn't be the Jackie I am now. She's not perfect by any means, but she's a helluva better person than she was." Jackie moved over to the table and chairs. She wiped each chair down with cleanser, and with the last swipe, the table was cleaned, good as new.

Eric stood back and admired their work. "You know we make a dynamic cleaning team. It doesn't even look like Tornado Jackie has been through here."

Jackie couldn't help but smile. They did make a great team. They always had. Why had she fought it so hard? She wasted so many years denying what she truly felt and wanted, and for what? And then when she and Jimmy finally divorced, she still didn't do the right thing. She should have been on the first plane to Charlotte. But she wasn't. It was almost as if she didn't want to be happy. She wondered just how many chances did one get.

Eric pulled out a chair and motioned to Jackie to sit down. "I don't know about you, but I'm going to sit right down on these clean chairs and take a rest. I got you beat by a few years. I was fifty-four last April."

"I remember also. April fifth. Let me see if there's any wine left to drink around here. I don't think I touched that last night. And I think I have some cheese and crackers too. I don't know about you, but I haven't had much to eat today, and I'm starving." Jackie went into the pantry and came back with a bottle of merlot and some crackers. She went over to the refrigerator and found some little rounds of cheese. "Just let me grab a couple of plates, glasses, and the wine opener, and you can do the honors, Mr. Henderson."

They sat around the table in companionable silence, sipping their wine and eating cheese and crackers. The house phone rang and they both looked at each other.

"I guess I better get that. Hello? Oh. Hi, Tony." Jackie smiled and turned her back to Eric as she took the call.

Eric heard Jackie stifle a genuine laugh and got up from the table and went into the keeping room. He stood and stared out the window. There was a security light on, and he could see the patio and the beautiful trellis full of roses. He looked at his watch. He hadn't realized it was past eleven o'clock. Jackie seemed to have forgotten him as she talked to her friend. He felt deflated, as if all the progress he'd made with her tonight had suddenly disappeared.

Jackie finished the call and came over to stand beside Eric. "That was Tony, checking up on me. I told him you brought me home."

"He seems to care about you a lot. I don't know many people who would have hung with you and your family drama like that. Like I said, he seems to be your prince in shining armor. But you're so easy to like, to love."

Jackie smiled at the compliment. "Well yes, I care about him too. He's a fine young man, not my prince though. He helps me out a lot at work. He's very tech savvy. We've gone out a few times, and he's a lot of fun. He reminds me of you, just a younger version. He's so kind and considerate. He's good-looking and single. So manly. A red-blooded woman would have to be out of her mind not to find him attractive."

She had a wistful look on her face as she looked out the window at her trellis. "I was thinking about giving him a chance earlier, before you blew the doors off the church. I was thinking it was time to let go of the past and move on with my life. Even Chrystal told me I needed to do that. If nothing else, last night showed me that too." Jackie gave a little sigh.

Eric turned slightly and tilted his head to the side. He bent down and kissed her lightly at the corner of her lips. It seemed she had made up her mind about them. Sadly, he said, "I guess I better go, and let you get some sleep. I hadn't realized it was getting so late."

"Do you really want to? Go, that is. It's not that late, and I didn't finish giving you the complete tour. We didn't follow the food trail down the hallway. You never know what might be waiting at the end."

"If I follow the food trail to your bedroom, do you know what will happen? I know what I want. Do you?"

Jackie didn't answer his question. She just turned and followed the sloppy odds and ends of stepped on food to her bedroom. "If you're coming, then be careful of the noodles. At least, I think they're noodles."

Eric caught her at the door to her bedroom. It was partially open. He turned her around to him. "I have to ask again. Do you know what you want? If I step through this doorway, there's no turning back. There's no fine young Tony or any other man in your life but me. Do you understand?"

"Yes, I understand. I want to let go of the past. I want a future. I don't want to be just half-way existing. I want to live. I'm tired of being afraid to love and be loved. I want you."

She took his hand and led him into her bedroom. She turned on the lamp beside the bed. "If you can ignore the mess, then give me a kiss. Not a peck on the cheek. Not a grandma kiss. I want a kiss that will wake me up. I've been asleep for almost fifteen years."

"Then be quiet so I can kiss you properly on those luscious lips of yours."

Eric moved to the bed and sat down. He pulled her down to his lap and gently took her face in his hands. He looked into her eyes and saw a sheen of tears starting to form. "Don't you dare cry on me! This is the beginning of the rest of our lives together. We will not start off with tears."

He kissed her then, and he put all the emotions that had been boiling away into that kiss. All the loneliness, the hurt, and even anger that he'd carried with him for over twenty years spilled out onto her lips. But it also contained all the exuberance of youth, all the love but with a seasoned mellowness that only experience could produce. He made her remember the excitement of the first time and gave her a promise of the best that was to come for the future. He took her mouth passionately, the same way he was going to take the rest of her.

"I love this green color on you, but this dress has got to go. It's just in the way right now." He unzipped the dress without moving her from his lap. As he slid the dress off her shoulders, he caressed and licked her exposed skin. "You can't know how long I've wanted to be able to do this." He caressed her soft skin and nuzzled at her shoulder. "I don't know what perfume you use, but I'm going to buy you a carload. It's driving me crazy. It's so sexy. I just want to lick every inch of your skin."

"I'm not wearing any perfume, but you can still lick every inch of me. I've been waiting just as long as you. So let's get on with the show." Jackie raised her hips so he could slide the dress off. She clutched his shoulders and then ran her fingers up and down his arms, his chest. "You feel like hot suede. All warm and smooth to the touch, but so strong. I've wanted to touch your skin since I first saw you again today."

Eric expertly removed her lacy bra and tossed it into the pile of clothes strewn around the bed. He turned her in his lap so she was straddling him. His lips easily targeted the warmth from her neck. He lifted each breast and placed an open-mouth kiss on her nipples, sucking gently. Jackie arched her back and pulled his head as close as it could get to her breast. She ran her hand over his beautiful head of reddish hair.

"You were always just perfect for me," said Eric. "I love these. They fit perfectly into my hands. I could kiss them all night, but there's so much more I want to do to you. Stand up. Let's take these pretty little panties off. There's not much to them. You must have known I was going to take them off tonight."

"Wait. I don't want to be the only one who's naked. You got to take something off too." Jackie stood up off Eric's lap. "Let me help you with this useless shirt. Those pants look to be straining over something big. Yeah, now, isn't this so much better?"

Eric tugged off his pants and tossed his shirt into a corner as Jackie sat back down on his lap. She ran her hands over his tight stomach. Her breasts gently swayed back and forth as she caressed his taut muscles. He wanted so badly to capture them and smother them with more kisses. But he also didn't want her to stop touching him. Every fingertip worked a magic over his skin that he had needed almost as much as his next breath.

She couldn't believe this man was here and he wanted her this much, still. The evidence was plain to see. She reached down farther and cupped him through his underwear. It had been so long, too long. Could she be what he wanted, what he needed? Did she still have enough of the good stuff? She started to feel self-conscious. She wasn't twenty-five—hell, not even forty-five—anymore. Things that used to perk up had fallen down. Her trim little waist had expanded to new dimensions. Eric had probably been with all sorts of beautiful young women over the years.

She suddenly pictured cute little Michelle in Eric's arms. What if he didn't like what he was seeing? Jackie knew she couldn't compete with a slim little thirty-year-old; not even a forty-year-old. She suddenly stopped touching Eric and stood up. She took her hands and tried to cover herself while sucking in her stomach.

Eric pulled her down to his lap again. She held herself back from him and moved her hands to cover herself again. He moved her hands to her sides. She turned her head away from him, but not before he saw a myriad of emotions crossed her face. He took his time, waiting for her to face him. Jackie chickened out and dropped her head.

"You're thinking too damn much," Eric told her. "I saw the questions in your eyes. I'm here because I want to be. Nobody is forcing me, and if I didn't like what I was seeing, I wouldn't be this rock hard right now." He ran his hand over himself and licked his lips.

Jackie heard a giggle. At first, she didn't know where that sound had come from. Then she laughed outright. It felt so good; it felt so right.

He had put her at ease just by being himself. This was what she loved about him. Eric joined her, and they fell laughing onto the rumpled bed.

"You looked just like LL Cool J doing that. But you're so much sexier and so much more mine. I want you. I love you. Even when I knew I shouldn't, I never stopped. Even when I said I didn't."

Eric sat up and finished taking off his underwear. "I'll just get rid of these too. They're trying to choke me to death, and I know you wouldn't like that. Now, back to this little piece of nothing you call panties." He slipped his fingers under the waistband and gently tugged. As he moved them down, he bent his head and placed a kiss on her stomach.

Jackie raised her hips, helping him get her panties off faster. He flicked them over his head and behind him somewhere and licked and nipped at her again. The insides of her thighs got a lot of attention, and then he moved higher still.

When he reached the apex of her thighs and licked her there, she thought she had died and gone to orgasm heaven. She hadn't had sex in over ten years, and it had certainly been longer still since she made love. She felt his hot moist breath on her most intimate lips, and she loved it. Jackie let out a moan that had been held back far too long. She grabbed at his shoulders to pull him even closer between her legs.

Eric took both her hands in his large hand and held on to them as he made love to her with his lips and tongue. Then he pulled her even closer by grabbing her hips and massaging her lush ass. She twisted, she turned, but he would not let her go. And she prayed he never would.

Her body rocketed off the bed. It was torture of the best kind. She pushed him away. She pulled him to her. Jackie didn't know if she would live through the pleasure he was giving her. She hadn't had an orgasm like this since … ever. She felt fractured, blown apart into a million little beautiful pieces. Her senses were scattered, and she fought to bring air back into her lungs. She now knew what they meant by a mind-blowing experience. Before she could completely come back into herself, Eric moved up and encircled her with his arms and kissed her deeply.

Breathlessly she said, "Let me love you the same way."

As she started to move, Eric said, "No, not this time. I'm about to come just from touching you. This first time, just let me inside you."

Jackie slowly nodded her head, but she said, "It's been a long time for me. I don't know if I can take all that." She reached between them and took a firm grasp of his engorged member.

"Yes, you can. You were made for me. I'll go slow and easy. Just tell me if you want me to stop."

He filled her slowly, inch by wonderful inch, until he was completely seated to the hilt. He rocked gently in and out getting her used to being filled by him again. She moaned his name.

He struggled to ask, "Are you okay? Do you want me to stop? Not that I could, but I would try. I would do anything for you."

She would have to be a complete fool to tell him to stop. This was more than she remembered. It was even more than she could have imagined, and she had a very creative imagination. "No, don't you ever stop," she gasped.

His body was hot and slick with sweat and heavy on hers, but it was a weight that felt so right. She pleaded with him for more, so he took her legs and wrapped them around his waist. She opened herself up even wider for him to go deeper. She ran her needy hands over his wide shoulders and his back and felt the tight muscles there. She used her freshly manicured nails to leave a trail of scratches on his back. Then she gripped his tight ass with a desperation and pulled him deeper still. She couldn't believe that this man was finally hers. No hiding, no secrets, no doubts.

He begged her, for what he didn't know—but he did know. He loved her, and there was nothing that could come between them now. It felt so good, words couldn't come close to describing it. He didn't know where he ended and she began. He was in so deep there was no going back. But they both knew what they were straining towards. It was like a tight coil, wrapping tighter and tighter with every thrust until finally it burst free from the momentum, a release so sweet that all they could do was savor it and find a little bit of heaven in the midst of it all.

Jackie didn't know how she could have been crazy enough to deny herself this. This man, God help her, was everything and a million more of everything else. Every nerve in her body concentrated into the one place they came together. Over and over, he gave her everything he had, and she was more than happy to greedily take it.

They moaned each other's names and reached a peak that was higher than Mount Everest. It sounded so lame, but she saw stars, nebulas, every celestial body in the universe. She was falling through a black hole, but it was filling her with a brilliant light, not never-ending darkness.

And he still didn't stop. It was as if he was marking her as his all over again, and this time, she would never forget. He couldn't stop now if his world was coming to an end. He knew if it did end, he was right where he wanted to be. He loved this woman, and for the first time in his life, he was absolutely positive she loved him just as much. This wasn't the end. No, this was just the beginning of what they had been seeking all their lives.

Much later, Jackie loaned Eric one of her caftans. Wearing it, he looked like an African prince, albeit one with too short of a robe. It stopped a little below his knees. They went back to the kitchen, and he made her an omelet out of whatever he could find in the refrigerator.

"I remember how good of a cook you are. This omelet is to die for." Jackie ate her food with enthusiasm. "Although I think a stale piece of toast on a napkin would taste just as good after what we just did." She smiled and stuck her tongue out at Eric.

"Are you sticking your tongue out in invitation? I think I still have a little stamina left. Just let me finish eating and I'll be ready for round two." Eric gave her another dazzling smile and continued eating.

Jackie laughed. "You mean round five or six, don't you? I lost count after the first couple of times. But seriously, I feel like the weight of the world has been lifted from me. I didn't want to hear a lot of the truth today, or I guess yesterday, since it's after midnight, but now I'm glad for everything that happened."

Eric finished his omelet and took a swallow of his juice. "I hated to see the tears in your eyes, but I think now there's a chance for everyone to heal. And I know just how embarrassing it must have been to have your mother see you in this light, but it takes that sometimes."

They talked about everything that had happened at the wedding and at Ms. Sylvi's house. There was no holding back. It was a catharsis that was long overdue.

Jackie stood up and took the dirty dishes to the sink. "Do you think Chrystal will be all right? She looked devastated."

"I really don't know. I feel so inadequate when it comes to understanding either of them. All these years, I thought of them as my children, but only in the sense of paternity. I never really got a chance to see them as people with everything that entails. You know, with their own personality, desires, and wants."

"Well, I raised them, and I'm just as perplexed. I've never really communicated well with Chrystal. There was always something missing there. I see now what I have been doing to her. I don't want to believe that I was that blind to it all but I know now and I can do something about it. But Royce, I thought we had a great relationship. I found out I don't know him as well as I thought either."

"Well, whatever happens now, we'll go through it together. I love you, and there's nothing you can do about it. By now, I'm sure you see that." Eric came over to the sink and almost picked Jackie up with the bear hug he gave her. "Now what was that tongue business you teased me with?"

Jackie laughed again, and her eyes filled with shiny tears of joy. "Okay. I teased you, and now I have to back it up with action. Take me back to the bedroom, and I'll see what I can do."

"You definitely got a deal. Let's go, and this time, I'll let the tears slide because I know they're tears of happiness."

The purpose of poetry

Well, it won't feed your family, that's for sure
So why do we hang all our hopes on this cure?
Searching through our hearts, cramped from pain
Hunched over paper or computers with a frozen brain

Wearing our feelings on our face, feeling insane
Forlornly looking through eyes opaque with shame
Trying to rhyme and count beats to a wordy flow
Hoping to garner an audience for our poetry show

If you look at the world and what one must do
To make a living, work hard, raise a family too
The purpose of poetry doesn't rank very high
But the right word with meaning makes one sigh

Reading the great masters, brings a smile to our face
Knowing others feel how it is to be in our place
Seeing exotic lands and even the regular humdrum
Is like savoring the flavor of a sweet, ripened plum

The purpose, as you vigorously shake your head,
The dusty musings of great thinkers long ago dead
Doesn't sound like much that should get you in a stir
But without poetry the world would be nothing but a blur

A place of no color, devoid of style, lacking grace
All grays and browns that lock you in a silent place
The purpose of poetry is to free us from that mold
It won't feed your family, but it sure feeds your soul

Barbara Combs Williams
A Remember Too Design

www.ingramcontent.com/pod-product-compliance
Lightning Source LLC
Chambersburg PA
CBHW022113170626
46808CB00002B/714